R0061347050

11/2011

JUST FRIENDS

JUST FRIENDS

•

Annette Mahon

AVALON BOOKS
THOMAS BOUREGY AND COMPANY, INC.
401 LAFAYETTE STREET
NEW YORK, NEW YORK 10003

PRINTED IN THE UNITED STATES OF AMERICA
ON ACID-FREE PAPER
BY HADDON CRAFTSMEN, BLOOMSBURG, PENNSYLVANIA

For all my readers on the Big Island, with aloha.
Mahalo for your support.

Chapter One

Kimo Ahuna stepped into the hospital. Reluctantly.

He took a deep breath and instantly regretted it. Why did hospitals all have that same smell? A combination of antiseptic and sickness, of hope and despair, it took him immediately back to places and times he never wanted to revisit. Busy, over-crowded wards; stifling heat; the smell of blood and sweat; the sound of people speaking in foreign tongues.

It was years ago now, but the memories were fresh as ever. Kimo and Jack Lyman, island boys on foreign soil, doing their part to help their country, and other starving countries.

Oh, yes, Kimo Ahuna and Jack Lyman had a lot

1

in common. More than friendship, more than their Hawaiian heritage. More even than their jobs in the flower industry, and their service in the National Guard. Unfortunately, among their shared experiences were hospitals.

And if Kimo was reluctant to step into a medical center, he knew Jack would be horrified to discover himself back in one of those antiseptic high beds with their sterile white sheets.

Kimo rubbed his hand across the lower part of his face and shook his head once as he headed across the lobby. A deep breath couldn't dispel the memories; it drew in too much of the astringent odor that was so intimately allied with them.

But Jack needed him.

Kimo scanned the lobby, willing himself to forget the past and think only of the future. He knew where to go from the directions he'd received over the phone. He just prayed he wasn't too late.

Ilima Lyman sat silently in the waiting room, her hands idle in her lap. She stared at the table before her, a large round one covered with an assortment of colorful magazines. Her twin lay in a room down the hall, halfway between life and death. Unable to do anything but think about her brother and his tentative hold on life, Ilima sat staring at the gaudy array, feeling guilty at her inability to actually do anything constructive. She'd been praying ever since she'd found him, but that lacked the kind of tangible results she craved.

The sound of someone repeating her name brought her out of her temporary daze. A tall man holding a duffel bag in his hand was stooping over her. He must have been there for a minute or two, and she hadn't even heard his approach.

"Kimo."

Ilima was so glad to see her brother's friend, she leaped out of her chair and threw her arms around him. "Kimo," she repeated. "You came."

"Did you doubt that I would?"

His voice was low and soothing. The doctor's had been too, but somehow not as comforting. And the doctor had not given her a warm hug.

"No. No, I didn't." Ilima released her brother's best friend, stepping back toward her chair. She was so glad he'd come. "Thank you."

Kimo stood before her for a moment. He shifted his weight from one foot to the other, then seated himself beside her. He grasped his hands together between his knees as he faced her. "Tell me what happened."

Ilima swallowed. It was still hard—almost too hard. Barely half a day since she'd found him, but those twelve hours had impacted her life in ways that were still to be resolved. She took a deep breath and willed her heart back to its normal beat. "I was out last night, with friends. We stopped for drinks—and talked. And talked."

She twisted her hands together, her fingers whitening with the effort. "It was pretty late when I got home. There were a lot of lights on, but I didn't think too much of that. Jack had trouble sleeping. . . ." Ilima had been staring at her hands, but now she raised her eyes to Kimo's. A sad grin touched her lips. "You know about that, I guess."

Kimo nodded, his lips set in a grim line. Yes, he did know about that. Another thing he and Jack had in common. Though Kimo had managed to overcome his problem, not having had a nightmare for over a year now. Jack hadn't been so lucky.

Ilima's eyes turned once again to her limp hands, held quietly in her lap. "I called to him. Laughed and told him he didn't have to wait up any longer, that I was home." A tear rolled gently down her cheek, but she didn't seem to notice. "There was no answer. He wasn't in the living room or the kitchen. . . . So I went to his room."

Ilima's voice choked on a sob. Tears fell into her lap now, forming little damp spots on her khaki shorts, leaving rainlike drops on her hands. She looked back up at Kimo.

"He built himself another room, you know. On the other side of the carport. Said he needed his privacy. But I know he was worried that his late nights were disturbing me.'' Her expression said what her lips did not. As if anything her beloved brother did could really bother her.

''Anyway, he wasn't in the house, so I went out to his room. He wasn't there either.''

Kimo handed her a tissue from the box on a side table. As if unaware of the tears slipping down her cheeks, she held the tissue in her hands, alternately crumpling and smoothing it until it began to shred between her fingers. With a deep sigh she resumed her narrative.

''He liked to go on long walks when he couldn't sleep, so I decided to wait up for him. I was kind of keyed up myself after my night out. And I'd had a lot of caffeinated drinks. I didn't think I'd be able to sleep either. So I turned on the television and found an old movie to watch.'' Her voice quieted even more, and her words came slower. ''It was almost dawn before I started to worry. That's when I went out to look for him. And . . .''

She couldn't go on. As tears streamed down her cheeks, she tried to wipe at them with the bits of tissue left in her hands. But the tortured tissue disintegrated into a flutter of white flakes that drifted across her lap and onto the floor.

Kimo reached for her. She was hurting. It made *him* hurt just to watch her. And all he could think to do was to pull her into his arms and offer comfort from that human touch. Sometimes a hug was worth more than gold.

Ilima continued to sob quietly into his shirt. Kimo just held her, his hand rubbing gently over her back. He sometimes held his small niece this same way when she was upset about something. Holding her calmly in his arms was the best way to get the little girl beyond the frustrations of being three years old and little in a world filled with larger, stronger people.

Just as it worked for little Mealoha, his technique worked on his best friend's sister. Ilima soon dried her tears and pulled away. Pink stained her cheeks as she realized she'd been sitting practically on his lap sobbing into his shoulder. Kimo didn't mind. But apparently Ilima did. She scooted quickly back into her own seat and pulled more tissues from the nearby box.

Kimo pretended not to notice while she wiped her eyes and generally attempted to make herself more presentable. He had sisters and knew that they disliked being watched when they were primping. And while this was different from putting on makeup or arranging a hairdo, pulling oneself together after a crying jag must surely fall under the same category. So instead, he concentrated on what she'd told him earlier on the telephone.

"You found him lying on the side of the road?"

Ilima nodded. Never would she forget that sight. The day was new and suffused with a pink glow. Mauna Loa rose up behind her, a dark shadow against a deep blue sky. The air was clear and fresh, almost chill. A beautiful dawn promising a beautiful day. What a tremendous contrast to the horror awaiting her at the edge of the road.

"I walked out to the end of our driveway and I could see something on the shoulder about a hundred yards away." Even the rosy dawn light hadn't been able to soften the jolt that still hit her when she saw again that dark lump beside the road.

Her voice dropped so low Kimo had to strain to hear.

"I thought it was some trash that had fallen from a truck." She swallowed heavily and blew her nose a final time. "I was going to go out and pick it up, to throw it away."

Kimo noticed that her back had straightened as she braced herself for what was coming. "But it wasn't old clothes, or a load of trash. It was Jack." She caught herself before she broke down again. "Just lying there."

She swallowed again, and her mouth grew tight with strain. "I should have looked for him as soon as I got home. Though I'm sure he wasn't there then." Her voice caught on the words as she once again pictured that mound on the side of the road. "Not when I pulled into the driveway. I would have seen him."

"Now stop that."

The sharp tone of Kimo's voice startled Ilima into looking up into his eyes. Her clear brown eyes were wide with surprise. Kimo had to admit that the intense nature of his statement had surprised him too. But she couldn't do this to herself. He could hear the doubt clouding her voice. She actually believed Jack might have been lying there injured when she returned home. And that she hadn't seen him.

"It's not your fault. It was an accident."

Kimo reached over to Ilima and grasped her shoulders in his hands. He couldn't let her go on thinking this way.

"Ilima. Please." Kimo's fingers ran lightly along her shoulders, bare in her sleeveless shirt. Her skin was soft and smooth, warm to the touch. "Ilima. We're alive, you and I. And right now, Jack is too. We have to stay strong for him. And you can't eat yourself up with guilt over an accident." His dark eyes burned into her lighter ones. "It was not your fault," he repeated, saying it slowly so that each word was distinct, sharp, and clear.

Ilima stared into his eyes, as though searching

for something there. Kimo didn't know if she found
it, but he could see the resolution in her eyes as
she reacted to his words. She straightened her
shoulders, and he released her, bringing his hands
back to his side.

''You're right. Jack will recover, and we'll have
to be here, in good health. For him.''

Kimo looked over at his best friend's sister. Like
Jack, who stood six feet tall, Ilima was tall, at least
five foot nine. She had dark hair, thick and wavy,
that she'd pulled back from her face with a ruffly
piece of fabric. But a halo of fluffy bits of the fine
strands stood out around her head like an aura, the
hairs closest to her head of a darker hue than the
longer strands that shone with streaks of reddish
gold from long exposure to the sun. The remarkable
hair set off a long face with strong features, and
intriguing uptilted brown eyes. Her eyes were beautiful, a clear, pale brown the color of apple cider.
Heavy lashes surrounded them, encircling her eyes
with a natural dark highlighting that created a mys-
terious and exotic look. A wide mouth and full lips
completed the picture of a very pretty woman.

However, at the moment, the very pretty woman
before him had dark circles under her eyes, eyes
reddened from lack of sleep and her earlier bout of
tears. Unless she made the effort to hold them

straight, her shoulders sagged as though with the weight of a heavy burden. Kimo was determined to take that burden from her.

"Come on. Let's go to the cafeteria. I left in a hurry and I'm starving. And I'll bet you could stand to have something as well."

Ilima didn't argue. She did, however, check her watch to be sure there was time before her next short visit with Jack. Apparently satisfied, she stood and followed him down the hall, stopping just long enough to tell the nurse where she could be found.

Kimo and Ilima sat in the hospital cafeteria, plates of half-eaten food before them. Ilima watched Kimo as he finished up his burger. In all her difficult life, this was the worst time she could remember, because her twin brother wasn't here beside her. Unlike most of her local friends, Ilima and Jack had no extended family. The only children of only children, they had been raised by their grand-parents, both now deceased. In all the various crises of their young lives, she and Jack had always had each other; now she was alone. To be able to have this man, Jack's friend, with her was so special it brought tears to her eyes. At least she wouldn't have to face this alone.

Blinking rapidly to clear her vision as well as to keep the tears from falling, Ilima took a sip of the surprisingly good coffee. She'd made a halfhearted attempt to eat a muffin, but had pretty much given up. She might as well settle for taking in more caffeine to help her stay alert and watch Kimo instead.

Above the edge of the cup she could observe Kimo as he finished his meal. A large burger, fries, fruit, dessert. A jumbo drink. A wry smile touched her lips. At least Jack's situation wasn't affecting everyone's appetite. Kimo was a handsome man, his large frame reflecting his Hawaiian ancestry. He needed a good appetite to keep up that tall, muscular figure. He was at least six foot two, and his shoulders were very broad, even broader than Jack's. Ilima wondered if he'd gotten them swimming, like her brother. And Kimo's skin had the rich bronzed look of someone who spent many hours outdoors in the subtropical sun. Also like her brother.

Ilima gave a weak smile when Kimo looked over and caught her eyes on him. The smile he returned caused her heart to turn over. He had a beautiful smile, slightly sad, which was to be expected under the circumstances. Ilima had met Kimo several times over the years, but only for brief visits. She'd always been busy with her share of the work and with her own friends, and so had not spent much time with him. But she had admired his athletic figure. And she'd always noted his charming smile.

Jack often said Kimo could charm the dentures off an old *mama-san*. Ilima had no trouble believing it.

Lost in her thoughts, Ilima didn't notice Kimo finish his meal and lean back in his chair.

Kimo wished for a more comfortable piece of furniture to relax in, but he had to admit the view was great. He and Jack had been buddies since their first days in the National Guard ten years ago. He'd been twenty then to Jack's eighteen, and at first he'd taken Jack under his wing, treating him like a kid brother. But the two men discovered numerous areas of common interest and quickly became fast friends.

Kimo had visited Jack often over the years. How was it he'd never noticed that Ilima was a darned attractive woman? More than that. Kimo frowned. Physical beauty was only part of her appeal. There was something about her—an ethereal quality that drew him to her and made him want to help and comfort her. Protect her. Most of all, he'd like to take that sadness out of her eyes. But at the moment, that was something only a miracle could accomplish.

A miracle! Kimo thought of something simple he could do that might bring her comfort.

"Ilima."

Ilima started slightly at his voice, but turned alert eyes toward him.

"After we leave here tonight, would you like to stop at the church and light a candle?" Kimo might not be an overtly religious person, but he'd been raised in the Catholic church like many another islander with a Portuguese ancestor. His mother liked nothing better than to light a candle for a person who wasn't feeling well, either physically or emotionally. She'd lit many a candle both for him and for Jack in the past.

Kimo didn't know if Ilima was a practicing Catholic, but he knew the twins had been raised in the church, just as he had been. Religion was a wonderful thing in times of stress, and it might be just what Ilima needed.

Ilima stared at Kimo for a moment. She thought of her grandmother, of the way she would walk up the church aisle before mass and kneel before the rows of candles. When they were children, it had been a special treat for Ilima and Jack to light one as well. She felt sure their grandmother, a sweet, kind woman, was in heaven right now. She would look out for Jack. And she would like it if Ilima lit a candle for him. Perhaps she'd light one for Grandma as well.

She smiled at Kimo, the first real smile he'd seen from her. "I'd like that."

*   *   *

The inside of the church was cool, a pleasant contrast to the late-afternoon warmth outside. Spots of color littered the floor as the sunlight streamed through the row of stained-glass windows that ran the length of the building. The bright double line of colorful glass saints watched impassively as Ilima and Kimo walked up the side aisle, to the bank of candles at the foot of the Virgin's statue. Their footsteps sounded loud, echoing in the quiet of the sanctuary. The rattle of paper and of coins hitting metal was even louder as Kimo put some money into the donation box.

Ilima lit two candles. Kimo hesitated a moment, then lit one as well. Then they moved into one of the pews and knelt together to say a prayer.

Ilima felt the peace of the church interior wrap around her like a comfortable old shawl. She'd become an irregular churchgoer in recent years, but in this time of crisis she had found herself praying. And this now seemed right, to be here, lighting a candle, saying a prayer. She remembered her grandmother doing the same thing when her grandfather was ill. She'd been young but had felt very grown-up when she got to light a second candle on her own. She'd knelt beside her grandmother then and recited her prayers. Even at such a young age she'd felt the peace the old woman had found. And now she found it again.

After several minutes of quiet prayer and contemplation, Kimo and Ilima rose as one and walked back outside. They stood for a moment on the steps beyond the door, enjoying the feel of the trade winds blowing across the portico. The sun was quite low in the sky now, the light growing softer. It was dim in the shade of the portico, and Kimo's face was shadowed when Ilima turned to look up at him. His strong, dark features could have been menacing in the encroaching dusk, but she found nothing but comfort there.

"*Mahalo,* Kimo."

Ilima smiled up at him, and Kimo was happy to see that smile. She appeared calmer now, and her eyes glowed in the low light. Her posture was tall and straight, and the tightness around her mouth was gone.

He returned the smile. "Anytime."

Ilima looked up the road, toward the hospital.

"You should go home." It was a gentle suggestion, offered in a quiet voice. Kimo didn't want to push. "Didn't the nurses suggest that when we left? You have to try to get some rest."

A wry smile tipped her lips. "Easy for you to say."

Kimo felt ashamed. He should know better than to offer such glib statements. "I'm sorry. I'll take you back to the hospital."

He'd taken a taxi from the airport to the medical center, but had driven Ilima's car to the church. She had insisted that she was too tired to get behind the wheel. He turned toward the parking lot, but a hand on his arm stopped him.

"Kimo. I'm sorry." Ilima looked up at him with those surprisingly pale eyes, so like her brother's. "You're right. I know I need to rest. They've been telling me that at the hospital too. All day. I just didn't think I could." Her eyes rested on his, and her hand squeezed his wrist in a gesture of friendship. "But maybe I can now."

Kimo covered her hand with his and returned the squeeze. He noticed that her hand was warm now, unlike earlier at the hospital. When he'd taken her hand then it had been as cold as ice. "Good. Let me take you home."

Ilima smiled. Another real smile. "I'd like that."

Chapter Two

Kimo spent the night in Jack's room off the carport. Ilima disappeared into her own room as soon as they arrived at the house, and didn't come out again. Not that Kimo would have noticed. Afraid to infringe in this difficult time, Kimo kept to himself in his friend's lonely room. The tidy bedroom with its sparsity of personal items bothered Kimo, and he found himself pacing up and down the length of carpet beside the bed. Finally spotting some paperback books on the lower shelf of the nightstand, Kimo sorted through a collection of mysteries and thrillers, finally settling on a well-read copy of a Tony Hillerman novel. He read until he fell asleep.

To his surprise, Kimo slept long and deep. Mental exhaustion apparently took more of a toll on the body than he had expected. He awoke when the sunlight hit his window, refreshed in body and in spirit, anxious to see how his friend was faring.

For Ilima, however, the night had been lengthy and restless. She woke at five-thirty, startled to realize that she had actually slept at all, not feeling as though she had. She splashed some water on her face, dressed quickly in the first thing at hand, and went outside, thinking to do some gardening to relieve the tension caused by her worry over her brother. The morning air was cool and damp, the plants dew-covered from a late-night rain. The earth smelled fresh and clean, and the flowers growing nearby added their heavy perfume to the thick, humid air.

Ilima and Jack grew tropicals for the cut-flower market, a business they'd learned from the grandparents who'd cared for them. Born of young parents, their mother a hippie from the mainland, their father young, spoiled, and rebellious, the twins had had an unstable childhood. When they were three, their mother suddenly decided she'd had enough of peace and earth and vegetarianism; she left them and their father without a backward glance and returned to her parents on the mainland. None of the Lymans ever heard from her again. Unemployed and immature, their father deposited the twins with his parents and went back to the bachelor life he'd left four years before. He'd died in a surfing accident on the north shore of Oahu at age twenty-five.

Their grandfather, a big man of Hawaiian, English, Russian, and Chinese ancestry, was a tall, taciturn man. He worked for the electric company where he was on call for emergencies at any hour of the day or night. When he was at home, he worked in the gardens, lovingly tending the same plants grown in old Hawaii—taro, ti, and ferns among them. But before the twins had reached their teens, he too had died.

In marked contrast to her husband, their grandmother was a small woman. Of mainly Portuguese and Japanese descent, she loved to grow flowers. Every week she cut her flowers for the twice-weekly farmers' market and took the buckets of blooms and her grandchildren with her to Hilo. In between, she tended the flowers in her gardens and looked after the regular clients she had on the mainland. Twice a month she took buckets of cut flowers to the graveyard, where she decorated the graves of her son, her parents, her in-laws, and eventually, her husband. And the twins were a part of all these activities, trailing along behind the old woman like tiny double shadows. She talked to them constantly, telling them stories and singing them songs as she worked.

Entering the gardens now, Ilima remembered her grandmother fondly as she bent to the task of weeding around the rows of ti plants that bordered the entrance to the flower gardens. The island weather might be ideal for growing flowers, but it was also perfect for fostering the growth of weeds. It took constant attendance to keep the various grasses and weeds from overtaking the commercial plants.

The early light was soft, the sun already warm on her back. She hadn't bothered with gardening gloves. The damp soil felt good on her bare fingers, and the earthy scent released with the weeds brought strong memories of her grandmother. Some of her happiest times had been spent right here in the gardens, pulling weeds with little bare fingers. With Grandma.

An hour later, pleasantly tired from working in the moist earth, Ilima returned to the house to clean up and get ready to leave for the hospital. Kimo was up, standing in the kitchen doorway, holding the door open for her to enter. Dressed in loose cotton shorts and a dark T-shirt, he was a refreshingly familiar sight in her topsy-turvy world, a sign that she was not alone after all. He'd obviously been busy while she worked. Pleasant cooking smells drifted to her nostrils through the open door.

"Good morning." At least she didn't have to force a smile. She was genuinely glad to see him.

He was such a good friend to come like this at a moment's notice.

"Good morning yourself. I hope you like pancakes."

She stopped halfway to the sink, noticing the array of pans and dishes, and the kitchen table set for two.

"You fixed breakfast? How sweet." How considerate too. Jack never cooked.

Kimo's eyebrows shot upward. "Sweet? Well, I don't know as how I can thank you for that. Sweet is hardly what one manly guy like me wanna hear."

Ilima smiled. Kimo and his humor were just what she needed at this troubled time. She turned from the sink, where she had been busy washing the mud from her hands and scraping the dirt from under her fingernails.

"Then how about . . ." Ilima paused, turning off the water and picking up a towel to dry her hands as she considered his statement. "Gee, what a great thing for a cool manly guy like you to do." She fluttered her lashes at him, then cocked one eyebrow as she looked to him for his approval.

"That's better." He answered in a mock serious manner, though Ilima could see the edges of his lips quivering with his desire to laugh.

He took the last of the pancakes from the griddle

and picked up the plate filled with golden disks a little larger than old-fashioned silver dollars. "Sit down, sit down," he urged, setting the plate on the table. He turned back to the stove, where he had another plate piled with fluffy scrambled eggs and a row of fried Vienna sausages. "I couldn't find any bacon, so I made these. I put out the syrup and butter—do you need anything else?" He stopped beside the table and looked down at her. "And do you want coffee or tea?"

Ilima's eyes widened in surprise. "Coffee or tea? You made both?"

"No. I made coffee, but I found a lot of tea bags in the cupboard, so I thought you might prefer tea. I didn't think Jack drank it," he added with a smile. "Anyway, I boiled some water. But you have so many different kinds I didn't know what you'd like."

Ilima had to blink several times to stop her eyes from brimming with tears. How had Jack been lucky enough to befriend this man? And now *she* had him to help her out in this trying time.

"I'd like some tea, please. Hibiscus, I think," she added when he opened the door of the cupboard where she kept her tins and boxes of assorted tea bags. She loved tea, found it comforting and soothing when times were troubling. And she kept at least a dozen varieties on hand, real teas and herbals, so that she could pick and choose as her mood dictated. She would have had coffee this morning, rather than put him to the trouble, but here he was offering to make it for her.

Ilima blinked again, the troubling moisture still bothering her eyes. She really needed to get more sleep. That, and the fact that in the past she had not had the best of luck with the men in her life, was making her too emotional this morning. Why couldn't she have met a good man like Kimo years ago, when she was younger and prettier and not so cynical?

Putting her maudlin thoughts aside, she smiled her thanks at Kimo as he placed the mug of tea on the table beside her. Then, although she wasn't hungry, she put a few of the small pancakes onto her plate.

"I hope you like the silver-dollar pancakes. They're my favorite," he said, helping himself to a dozen or so of the miniature pancakes. He covered them with syrup, then added eggs and sausage to his plate, urging some on Ilima as well.

Ilima accepted small portions of each, mostly to be polite. It was so nice of him to go to all this trouble; how could she refuse to eat? And it did smell good, so maybe her appetite would grow with each bite. She'd make an effort.

"I've never had such small pancakes before."

''Really?'' Kimo stopped pouring syrup to glance up at her. ''My mother always made these little ones for us kids. Then she'd make the bigger ones for the adults. But I like these better,'' he added, folding a whole flaky pancake soaked in butter and syrup onto his fork and then carrying it to his lips.

Ilima stifled a smile and the urge to call him on this Peter Pan aspect of his nature. There was something childlike about Kimo, and it was what made him the person he was. A large part of his charm was that boyish imp so visible in his laughing eyes.

With a start, Ilima realized that Kimo had finished chewing and was speaking.

''At home I sometimes add bananas and fine-chopped macadamia nuts. But I didn't find any here, so I made them plain.''

Ilima swallowed what she had in her mouth and took a sip of her tea. The sweet, fragrant liquid soothed her throat and warmed her belly. But she looked embarrassed. ''I need to restock the kitchen. We've been so busy, I've hardly had time. The weather's been so nice,'' she explained, ''and I usually wait to shop on the days when it rains and I can't work outside.''

Kimo put down his fork and frowned at her. He picked up his coffee cup but didn't take a sip.

"You've been working too hard. You and Jack both. He should be taking better care of you. You're way too thin."

Ilima's eyes flared and her head went back as if she'd been hit.

Kimo saw her reaction and quickly replaced his coffee cup. But her response came before he could act or explain.

"Jack doesn't take care of me."

He looked at the proud tilt of her head, the thin line of her lips. He stood and moved to stand beside her. His hand rested lightly on her shoulder, and his voice was soft and urgent. "I'm sorry. I didn't mean that the way it came out; I really didn't." He went down on one knee beside her chair, so that he could look into her eyes.

She stared back at him, the only pancake she'd eaten turning to stone in her stomach. He was just like other men after all. But the realization was worse, somehow, because she'd believed, however briefly, that he was different.

Her eyes dropped to her plate, and her mouth set in a tight, grim line. A gentle, caring man—one who was also a "cool manly guy"—was a myth after all.

"Ilima, please look at me."

Kimo's voice, low and compelling, reached toward her. His fingers, light on her chin, turned her head toward him. She raised her eyes, slowly, reluctantly, and he took his hand away.

Kimo hung his head and shook it slowly from side to side. Then he raised it again and met Ilima's gaze. An incipient grin tugged at the corner of his lips. "Listen, Ilima, just tell me to shut up. Everything I try to say comes out wrong. I've got my foot in my mouth up to my knee already. All I really meant to say was that I think both you and Jack look like you've been neglecting yourselves. You both work too hard."

Ilima's lips spread, a mournful grin being pulled reluctantly into place. "Okay. I know that you meant well. You're forgiven." She put her hand over his, which still rested lightly on her shoulder. "Now get back over to your own side of the table and finish eating this wonderful breakfast you made."

Kimo pushed himself to his feet and shot off a smart salute. "Yes, ma'am." He marched around the table to his partially eaten breakfast and executed a perfect turn before sitting down.

Ilima had to laugh, and the laughter released any tension left from their brief confrontation. "At ease, soldier."

Grinning back at her, Kimo proceeded to finish his breakfast. He asked her what she'd been doing outside, and they talked easily about the gardens for the rest of the meal. Without actually vocalizing it, they made a mutual decision to keep the conversation away from Jack. They both knew that they would discuss him more and at length. But both also knew it would be better to do it later.

Within an hour, breakfast was over, the kitchen was cleaned up, and they were once again in Ilima's car, this time heading toward the hospital. The start of the half-hour drive was quiet.

Ilima finally broke the silence. As though remembering Kimo's earlier words about their working too hard, she launched into an account of Jack's recent days.

"You were right earlier, you know. Jack's been working too hard the last few months. Just working all the time." She decided to ignore his charge that she was also working too hard. "And he's had terrible insomnia, worse than ever. He goes out at night and walks for hours. I told you he made that room for himself out on the other side of the carport, so he wouldn't disturb me. He never said so, of course, but I know that was the reason."

She stared out the window for a moment, not even seeing the rows of houses they passed. "He wouldn't ever say what was bothering him, but he just wasn't the same after that last mission the

Guard had in Africa.'' She glanced at Kimo. It was possible she could learn more from him than she ever had from Jack. ''I wondered if it had to do with that bombing incident when you two were wounded. But he swears it's not that.''

Kimo agreed. ''I'd believe him there. He wasn't badly hurt in that attack.'' Unlike himself. He was the one who'd had nightmares about exploding buildings disintegrating around him, roofs falling while he lay helpless below, unable to move.

He blinked back the memories, trying to concentrate on the road ahead. ''He saved my life, coming back in after he'd been thrown free, and digging through the rubble. I had a few nightmares about collapsing buildings, but Jack said he didn't.''

In fact, Jack had never admitted to *any* nightmares. He had told Kimo about the insomnia. And Kimo had a theory of his own.

''Seeing the way war had torn up the area—that was hard. The people starving. The children especially . . .''

And the adults who would steal the food they were trying to distribute; steal it from the needy women and dying children, to feed the still healthy guerrilla fighters. Or sell it on the black market.

Kimo tried not to remember those times; Jack apparently couldn't forget them.

Ilima accepted Kimo's surmise with a nod. ''He

never would talk about the time in Africa, and since I knew he'd been wounded I didn't press him. But I thought it might be something like that. I watched the spots they did on the news, and it was bad enough just seeing it on television. And Jack's always had a tender spot for children.'' Ilima frowned. ''I wish I could get him to date someone, maybe find a nice woman to marry. Then he could have children of his own. I know he'd make a good father.''

''He'd like being an uncle just as well,'' Kimo said with a grin. ''Last time we talked, Jack said he thought you were spending too much time out here alone. Said he wished you would date more.''

Ilima voiced her surprise. ''Jack said that?'' He'd never mentioned anything of the sort to her. ''Though now that you mention it,'' she continued, ''he did introduce me to a Ray Ikeda a few weeks ago. Claimed they were old friends from the Guard, though I never heard him mention him before. We all went out to eat, and Jack made an excuse to leave early. Ray had to take me home.'' She shook her head, wondering what her brother had been thinking. ''He must have been trying to set us up.''

Kimo grinned. ''And did it work?''

''No.''

The answer came so quickly, Kimo took his eyes off the road momentarily to glance over at her. His brows came together, almost meeting over his nose. "Did he make a pass?"

"Oh, no." Ilima almost giggled at the thought, and the absurdness of the suggestion came through in her voice. "Ray was a nice man, about two inches shorter than me, stocky, with horn-rimmed glasses. He's a financial planner, and that was about all he seemed interested in." Her smile widened. "In a word, he was boring with a capital *B*."

Kimo returned her grin. The thought that Jack's arrangement didn't work out made him surprisingly happy.

Ilima's brief spurt of fun quickly fled. "I feel bad now. I had no idea he was so concerned about my still being single. I thought the two of us did very well together, and we have each other for company. I've had such poor luck with dates in the past, I just haven't wanted to bother. Maybe if I wasn't so selfish he wouldn't have been out walking so late."

"You can't do this, Ilima." His voice came out harsher than he had intended, and he softened it. "You are not to blame about any of this. It was an *accident*. Even if you were there, chances are he would have gone out anyway. And you couldn't have done anything from inside the house if you *were* at home. And you were out on a date, which is just what he wanted you to do."

Ilima blinked and her brows drew together. "I wasn't on a date."

It was Kimo's turn to be surprised. "I thought you said—"

"I said I was out with friends. Three other *women* friends and I went to a baby shower for an old classmate Sunday afternoon. We hadn't seen each other for so long, we went out for drinks afterward and then continued on to someone's house. We talked until late, and it was after two when I got home."

"You have to have a life of your own." Kimo removed his hand from the steering wheel for a moment, reaching over to touch Ilima's hand, which was lying on the seat between them. "You did everything you could, Ilima. Just remember that."

Ilima looked ready to protest, but by then they were turning into the hospital parking lot. She let it go, instead turning her attention to helping him find an empty parking space.

The day passed much as the day before, with the exception that the emotional level was a notch lower. The initial shock of the accident had passed, and the doctor assured Ilima and Kimo that Jack was doing well. Although his head had been hit hard enough to cause the coma he was in, there was no swelling of the brain, the major worry in a coma situation. The doctor had hopes that he would soon come out of it. His other injuries were minor, a broken leg being the worst.

Ilima felt calmer on this second day of her vigil. She credited Kimo with helping her achieve this state. He helped keep her distracted during their time in the waiting room, and brought her candy bars and cups of tea. "To keep your strength up," he told her.

And several of Jack's friends stopped by to lend their support. Their presence also helped, even though none of them stayed for long. They'd seen the report of the accident in the newspaper and had cared enough to stop at the medical center. Ilima was touched by their concern.

Over lunch in the hospital cafeteria, Kimo brought up the Lymans' business, which was being neglected for the time being.

"What are you going to do about the farmers' market? It's tomorrow, isn't it?"

"Is it Wednesday already? Oh, my." Ilima moved her shoulders in a small shrug. "I just won't go in tomorrow."

Kimo's eyes drilled into hers. "You do real good business there, don't you?"

"We do. It's great, business-wise. I have some

regulars too, who come every week and buy—for offices and restaurants. But I want to stay here. Jack might wake up at any time. I wouldn't want to miss being here when he does.''

Kimo nodded. He understood that. "I didn't mean for you to go. But it is an important part of your business. So if you'll get up at dawn with me, we can pick the flowers and I'll do the market. I can use Jack's truck.''

This last was said in the manner of a question, his eyes seeking permission from her for his suggestion. Ilima felt the warm dampness of tears behind her scratchy eyelids. The lack of sleep was affecting her in many different ways; Kimo's small kindnesses had her close to tears. She grasped his hand, holding it briefly in hers.

''It's a date.''

Once again, Kimo and Ilima stopped at the church on their way home. They each lit a candle, and felt better for it.

Ilima pondered the power of early religious training as they drove back toward Pahoa. While her grandmother had been devout, Ilima herself had attended church only sporadically in the past few years: Christmas and Easter, the odd wedding or funeral, sometimes on Mother's Day. Yet suddenly, she found that the simple act of lighting a candle and saying a prayer brought her a tremendous amount of comfort.

She decided to share her thoughts with Kimo, asking his opinion of this phenomenon.

''I don't know,'' he admitted. ''I noticed the same thing. I don't go to church every Sunday, but I found myself praying as soon as you called and told me about the accident. I guess those old parochial school habits are hard to break.''

Ilima nodded. She'd begun to pray the instant she'd seen Jack crumpled at the side of the road. ''I may have to rethink my position on religion.''

''It's a good thing to have in a crisis,'' Kimo commented.

By the time they reached the house, Ilima was visibly wilting. Both the emotional strain of Jack's injury and the fact that he was still unconscious were taking a toll on her stamina.

Kimo helped her into the house, directing her into the bathroom. ''Fill the tub, put in some bubble stuff or oil or whatever it is you women use, and just soak. It will help you relax. I'll fix something for dinner and then you can go straight to bed.'' He leaned close to look into her bloodshot eyes. ''You need a good night's sleep or you won't be much help when Jack does wake up. And we have to get up early tomorrow to pick the flowers.''

Ilima gave a faint smile. "I almost forgot. Again. Time has gotten all messed up for me these last two days." She glanced out the windows, checking the sky for any sign of rain. The sky behind the mountains was turning purple as the sun went down, but there was still plenty of light. "Maybe I should do some picking now."

Kimo took her by the shoulders and turned her back toward the bath. "No. You're just about wiped out. We'll do it together in the morning."

Ilima raised her eyebrows, but didn't argue. She hated it when people told her what to do. But she *was* tired.

When she came out of the bathroom a half hour later, she was relaxed and warm, her cheeks tinted pink from the steam of her bath. She'd pulled on an old faded muumuu, a shapeless but comfortable dress that would do until it was time for bed. An herbal fragrance reminiscent of rain forests and tropical gardens drifted into the kitchen with her.

"Umm." She sniffed appreciatively. "What smells so good?"

Kimo looked up from his place in front of the stove. He wanted to say that she did, but decided that way led to trouble. She sure did look terrific, though, with damp curls framing her face, and her cheeks all rosy from the heat of the bath.

But he played it safe and confined his remarks

to the food. "Oh, just a few things I threw together."

He continued to stir the contents of the large frying pan, adding another dollop of *shoyu* for good measure. "You're just in time. Have a seat."

As he finished speaking he turned off the stove, lifting the pan to a pad on the counter. While Ilima sat at the already set table, Kimo scooped rice onto two plates, then heaped the aromatic mix of meat and vegetables on top of it.

Within minutes, they were sitting at the table with their meal before them, steaming cups of chocolate beside them.

"I've heard chocolate and hot milk are both good sleep aids," Kimo said. "So I thought a cup of hot chocolate should be helpful."

"I guess I'm willing to try anything at this point," Ilima admitted. She took a forkful of vegetables and chewed carefully. "This is very good. I don't think I would have had the energy to cook anything for myself."

"Then it's lucky thing you got me, eh?"

After a shared laugh, they ate in companionable silence. There seemed little to say to each other at this point, since they'd spent the whole day together. Yet it was a comfortable silence. Just the fact of being there, two of them, united by their friendship for Jack—it was enough.

Chapter Three

Kimo's home remedy of a hot bath and a cup of hot chocolate seemed to work. Ilima slept well, arising in the morning refreshed and ready to meet the day—even though the day had not yet begun. It was still cool from the *mauka* winds that blew through the night, the air heavy with humidity. The sky was lightening as the sun reached up to the horizon.

Ilima dressed quickly and headed outside. She found Kimo already in the carport, the clippers and buckets they needed for cutting the flowers ready and waiting.

They worked quickly and efficiently, cutting and grouping the flowers according to type. Not that there wasn't time for some fun. Kimo was a natural clown, and he wouldn't let Ilima be the sober, serious person she usually was. He found ways to make her laugh, once pretending to catch his hand in a spider's web that stretched its symmetrical lines of silk some two feet between the rows of colorful ti plants.

"Save me, Ilima, save me," he called out in a melodramatic voice. "My fingers are going to be Ms. Spider's lunch."

Ilima couldn't help her laughter. "And what makes you think it's a *Ms.* Spider?"

Removing his hand, which Ilima noted had not really caught in the beautiful filaments at all, he pointed to the egg sac securely attached at one end of the large web. "Actually, it's probably *Mrs.*"

Ilima gazed at the intricate web, sparkling with its morning coat of dew. It was a beautiful example of nature's art. "I hate to tell you this, but Mrs. Spider is going to have to go." She frowned as she looked over the pathway, blocked by the web. "I wonder if it's been here long. I haven't been out much, with Jack and all. . . ."

Kimo hurried to steer the conversation away from Jack. He'd enjoyed seeing Ilima laugh, getting her to relax enough for the worry lines around her eyes to disappear. But mention of Jack quickly brought them back.

"Here, I'll dispose of Ms. Spider," he announced. He closed his gloved hand over the large spider splayed out in the center of the web, twisting his wrist to wrap the web around his closed fist and thus clear the pathway. With thumb and forefinger he grabbed hold of the sticky egg sac. "Where's your compost heap? I'll just set her there to get a new start."

Ilima pointed the way, staring after him in bemusement. Jack would have killed the spider on the spot. She herself hated to kill anything except centipedes—she could barely repress a shudder at the thought of those creatures—but she would have. They couldn't have the webs closing off the paths between the rows, and there was something eerily terrifying about walking into one of those silken nets when the light was dim or she just wasn't paying attention.

But for Kimo to relocate the spider . . . Ilima had to smile at that. He must have been one of those little boys who was fascinated by insects. Did he put caterpillars in jars so he could watch them turn into butterflies, and catch grasshoppers in his little hands? It wasn't hard to imagine him as a small boy, lying on his stomach in the grass to watch the ants and the earthworms and whatever else might be crawling there.

Ilima was still smiling over the image of Kimo as a child as she walked alongside the tall green stalks of red ginger. The ginger had been her grand-mother's favorite, though she had grown a little of everything—bird of paradise, anthuriums, red ginger, and torch ginger. Grandma liked to put together mixed bouquets, and that was still her grandchildren's specialty. But they had diversified, adding more varieties and a few of the newer, more exotic types of flowers.

Ilima loved the red ginger too. It was one of her favorite places to work when she wanted to think. She could feel Grandma's presence here near her favorite plants, and just being here brought a certain peace.

She was leaning in, slightly off balance as she cut a long stalk, when she felt an abundance of damp drops falling on her. Surprised by the rain on what had seemed a clear morning, but used to tropical showers, she finished cutting the stem before looking up—right into Kimo's grinning face.

Ilima was so surprised by his sudden appearance, she almost fell over into the tall plants. How could such a large man move so quietly?

But she recovered quickly, straightening up and grabbing one of the tall leaf stalks. She flicked it toward him, showering him with wet droplets. Dark spots bloomed on his black shirt, matching the ones that had appeared on her own blue sweatshirt after the artificial shower.

"Ahhh. You want to play rough, huh?"

For a few minutes, they chased each other down the long row of red ginger plants, grabbing wet leaf stalks and creating their own kind of "rain." Their shouts and laughter competed with the early morning birdsong, and drowned out the traffic noises that drifted back from the highway. By the time they settled down and returned to their cutting, the morning was bright, the sun above the horizon. Its warm rays shone on their thoroughly dampened shoulders, warding off the chill of the wet fabric.

Glancing at her watch, Ilima cast a quick look over what they'd collected, declaring it enough. She was beginning to regret her earlier playfulness, wondering what had gotten into her. She hadn't done anything so childish since her teens. Maybe even before then.

Seeing Ilima's sudden change of mood, Kimo hurried off toward the house, citing the need to start breakfast.

By the time Ilima had gathered the money box and receipt book, and changed her wet shirt for a dry one, breakfast was ready and waiting. This morning it was scrambled eggs with Portuguese sausage and cold glasses of orange juice. He'd boiled water for her tea and made some instant coffee for himself.

"Not as much time to cook this morning," Kimo explained.

Ilima put some of the fluffy eggs into her mouth, chewing in appreciation. Kimo was a better cook than she was. Her scrambled eggs always came out heavy and overdone.

"Oh, Kimo. You're spoiling me something awful. How will I ever go back to waiting on Jack?"

Kimo laughed. "You'll just have to retrain him, sweetheart. Teach him to help out around the house."

The endearment caused Ilima's heart to skip a beat, even though she knew it was uttered unconsciously, a meaningless term he might use with any woman. Charming, carefree Kimo. She'd often heard her brother talk about Kimo and how the women seemed to flock to him. Now that she knew him better, she could understand why they did.

Taking a sip of her orange juice, Ilima scolded herself for the way she was letting Kimo's presence get to her. He was here because of Jack; her presence was incidental. She had no intention of becoming one of those women who chased after him.

With determination, she turned the conversation to business.

"I'll write down the prices of the different flowers for you. . . ."

*   *   *

It seemed strange, arriving at the medical center on her own. In just two days, Kimo had insinuated himself into her life in such a way that she missed him already after less than an hour apart. It made such a difference, having someone there beside her when she entered the hospital, and later, when she sat for hours outside the intensive care unit.

And when she heard that Dr. Kodani wanted to see her . . . Then she *really* wished Kimo were there to hear the news with her. She pushed away the sudden urge she felt to have her hand cradled in Kimo's larger one. But she dearly wished for his steadying presence beside her.

The doctor led her into his office, to a chair facing his desk. There was a second man already in the room, sitting on a chair against the wall, but Ilima was so focused on the doctor and what he would say that she didn't even notice him.

Dr. Kodani stood before her, half sitting on the edge of the desk, his hands clasped loosely together before him. His expression was earnest, his eyes full of compassion. "I'm afraid your brother took a downward turn last night."

Ilima's eyes widened. What little color there was in her face rapidly departed, leaving her pale, the dark purplish marks under her eyes showing up in stark contrast. Her hands tightened on the arms of her chair, and Dr. Kodani reached out a steadying hand. Her stomach already felt as if it held a lump of cement; just being called into the doctor's office was enough to cause that. Now her lungs seemed to clog so that she could scarcely get a breath. "Did he . . . ?" She couldn't bring herself to say the word.

"No, he's all right." The doctor, a kindly older man with a quantity of white hair, patted her hand, hastening to reassure her. "However, his blood pressure dropped very suddenly last night. That's very dangerous for a patient in a coma, and in his case was very unexpected. There is some indication that his IV medication was tampered with. That's why Detective Fernandez is here to talk to you." Dr. Kodani indicated the second man in the room, who had risen and was now standing at the side of the doctor's desk. Ilima turned to see a man about Kimo's age, perhaps a little older.

"We're very concerned, of course, about this occurrence," Dr. Kodani continued, "and we're conducting an investigation of our own. But since your brother was the victim of a hit-and-run accident, we felt it prudent to call in the police as well." He turned briefly toward the detective, then returned his fatherly gaze to Ilima. "But don't you worry. Your brother's condition has stabilized. He will be just fine. We expect him to come out of the coma soon."

He patted Ilima on the shoulder, then seemed at a loss as to what else he could say. So he nodded at Ilima, then at Detective Fernandez. "I'll just leave you two alone to discuss this then," he said, heading for the door.

Now, upset and confused, Ilima turned to Detective Fernandez, who offered his hand for a quick, businesslike shake. A sincere smile and a commiserating look in his warm brown eyes made Ilima take to him at once. She felt herself relaxing just a little. His smile was warm, friendly.

"Mel Fernandez," he said, settling into a chair beside hers. "I think we were at St. Joseph at the same time," he added, mentioning the local Catholic high school.

Ilima blinked at him, then smiled in recognition. "Mel. Yes, I do remember you now. You were ahead of us in school, though. I'm surprised you remember me at all. We were lowly freshmen when you were a senior and the star of the basketball team."

Mel shrugged, taking the chair opposite Ilima in front of Dr. Kodani's desk. He didn't want to tell her that it was only because there weren't that many twins at the school that he remembered her and Jack. She'd changed a lot since high school, her thin, gangly body having filled out in a very agreeable fashion. Her face had matured too, the baby fat in her cheeks replaced by a beautiful and dramatic profile. He remembered the pale brown eyes, unusual in the multitude of Polynesian and Asian races in the islands, but definitely appealing.

Mel pulled his mind back to business. He was not only a married man, but the father of a brand-new son, and he shouldn't be thinking about how attractive she was. He cleared his throat.

"The doctor feels fairly certain that your brother's medication was tampered with during the night. The hospital is checking into it right now. We'll be working with them on that." Mel consulted the small notebook in his hand. "Tests will take a few days. In light of this, we'll be conducting a further investigation into Jack's accident the other day. Can you think of any reason why someone would deliberately want to harm your brother?"

Ilima thought she now realized the meaning of *shell-shocked.* Surely it was what she felt right now: numb, feeling as though she were caught in a dream. The accident had been bad enough, but she'd never thought it anything but an accident. The perpetrator had not stayed around afterward, but that was not unusual these days. Especially if the driver had been drinking. No, she'd never entertained the thought that someone had deliberately tried to harm her brother.

"Jack? No one would want to harm Jack." She tried to pull together her shattered thoughts. "He doesn't socialize much, but the friends he has are good friends."

An image of Kimo fluttered across her mind. Yes, Jack might not have a lot of friends, but the ones he had were loyal.

"He was . . ." Deliberately she changed her terminology. "Jack *is* a workaholic. He gets up at dawn and works in the gardens until it gets dark. He doesn't have much time for friends."

"How about people he hired to work with him? Anyone terminated, anything like that? Maybe some hard feelings?"

Ilima thought that over. "I don't think so. We do hire people all the time. Most of them don't last long. It's hard work, and out in the sun, stooping over a lot of the time. And we can't afford to pay more than minimum wage. But I don't recall that there were ever any hard feelings over any of it."

She pursed her lips as she continued to think it over. Mel remained silent, letting her remember in her own time. Finally she shook her head.

"No, I can't think of anyone who might have held a grudge. Most of the guys I remember left because they quit. I don't think we've fired anyone for years."

"Why was he out on the highway at that time

of the night? Or morning, rather?'' he corrected himself.

He still held his notebook, but he hadn't added any more information to it. His eyes, caring and considerate, stayed on Ilima's.

Ilima brushed her hair out of her face, wishing she'd thought to pull it back this morning. ''Jack had terrible insomnia. It started after that last Guard mission in Africa. It was a humanitarian mission. They were supposed to pass out food and help protect ordinary people from the fighting gangs. He wouldn't ever talk about it, but he and his friend Kimo were injured. One of the buildings they were in was bombed. He's never been the same. His friend Kimo told me it had to do with seeing the results of the war, especially the effects on the children.'' A sad smile graced Ilima's lips. ''Jack has always had a tender spot for kids.''

''Did he take sleeping pills?''

Ilima shook her head. ''No. He refused to, even though his doctor recommended it. He said too many guys in the service got hooked on drugs when they started out taking something like that. For pain, or sleeping, he figured it was all the same; you start out taking a few for a good reason, and then you get hooked and start looking for the illegal stuff.''

Mel nodded. He was beginning to form a picture

of the kind of man Jack Lyman was. "What about friends in the Guard?"

Ilima shook her head again. It seemed to be all she could do, and it probably wasn't helping him at all. "I don't really know them, except casually. Except for Kimo, and he's from Maui. I did meet a Ray Ikeda a week or so ago. But he was just a nice guy, and we all had dinner together. I think Jack was trying to set us up."

Mel grinned. "Didn't work, I take it?"

"No." Ilima laughed. "He was nice, but very boring. Kimo would know more about Guard friends, though. He's working at the farmers' market for us this morning, but he'll be coming here afterward." She pushed the hair back out of her face again. "He flew in from Maui as soon as he heard. He's staying in Jack's room, in fact."

Mel made a note of Kimo's name and what Ilima remembered of his home address, then shut his notebook. "If you think of anything else, or anyone else who might have left your employ angry, please let me know." He handed her his card. "Just leave a message for me at the station if I'm not there, and I'll get back to you."

Business over, Mel got two cups of coffee from the machine at the end of the hall. Then he sat with Ilima in the waiting room and reminisced for a while. Their high school memories differed quite a bit, due no doubt to the gender difference as well as the three-year difference in their ages. But they'd had many of the same teachers, including Mrs. Yamaguchi for chemistry, and Sister Malia Damien for English and chorus.

"I wasn't very good at chemistry," Ilima admitted. "One day in lab I mixed up something that must have been a stink bomb. We had to evacuate that whole side of the building." At the time she'd been terribly upset, but now the memory brought a smile to her lips.

Mel laughed. "I did well in math, so chemistry was a breeze for me. It was English I had problems with. Sister Malia Damien was always getting after me. She thought I wasn't doing the reading, but I was. I just didn't know how to do the kind of writing she wanted, I guess."

Ilima nodded, her lips tipping up in a smile. "Jack had that same problem. I used to write two papers for every assignment, one for me and one for him."

"And he helped you with chemistry?" Mel smiled his understanding. He could see the sadness creeping back into Ilima's eyes. Their talk had brought her mind back to her brother and his current situation.

Mel reached over, touching her arm lightly to

offer comfort. "The doctors seem confident that Jack will be all right."

"I know. I just wish he'd wake up, so that I could know for sure. And now this . . ." Her eyes grew bright with unshed tears. She blinked furiously to hold them back, calling up a wavery smile to thank Mel for his concern. "Jack wouldn't hurt anyone. I don't know why anyone would want to harm *him*."

"We'll find out what's going on. Try not to worry." Mel knew that it was a trite thing to say, but it was all he could offer for now. With assurances that he would be in touch, Mel left the hospital.

Kimo found Ilima in a contemplative mood when he arrived back at the hospital a little past noon. He was so glad to see her it scared the happy bachelor in him. She seemed so fragile and so sad that he plunged right into an account of the morning's activity, including a large number of greetings and well wishes from the other vendors.

He was winding down when he realized that Ilima was even more subdued and emotional than she had been when he'd arrived two days ago. Once again her shoulders were slumped over in dejection. Her color was not good; she was much too pale, even her lips leached of their deep rose, now a pale, lifeless pink. And around the base of her chair were bits and pieces of white tissue. He knew what that meant. When she was agitated, she played with the tissues, twisting and shredding them between restless fingers. Confirmed bachelor or not, he felt a twinge in his chest.

"What's wrong?"

Ilima's eyes met his and she blinked. He wondered if she'd heard anything he'd said. But before he could say more she clutched her hands tightly together and began a recitation of the morning's events. She started out with her talk with the doctor, told him about Jack's blood pressure, and about Det. Mel Fernandez and his questions.

Kimo listened intently. Jack was basically a loner, but he was also a businessman, and it was impossible to do business in a void.

"And you can't think of anyone who might have fought with Jack?"

Ilima shook her head. "I've been thinking about it ever since I talked to Mel. I haven't been able to come up with a thing." She reached for a tissue, more to have something to do with her hands than because she needed it. "He asked about Guard friends, and I said he should ask you . . . But I didn't think there would be anybody there that would dislike him enough to try to kill him." She fumbled in her purse for the card Mel had given her. "He wants you to call him."

Kimo frowned as he thought about Jack's accident. "So they feel it wasn't an accident after all." His voice was soft, almost as though he were just talking to himself, thinking out loud. He shook his head.

"It doesn't make sense. You're right; Jack doesn't have any enemies. He doesn't get really close to people, so he just doesn't get that emotionally involved with anyone. He has lots of acquaintances, but not too many close friends."

Ilima nodded at this description of her brother. To Mel it might sound like a harsh description. But her brother was a wonderful, caring man. He just didn't make friends easily.

"I didn't understand this before, when I thought it was just an accident," Ilima said. "I mean, how can someone just leave a person lying on the side of the road that way? Still, you do hear of that kind of thing happening these days. But now, I really don't know what to think." She turned bleak eyes on Kimo. "Except that I'm scared. I don't know what happened to Jack, and he can't tell us. And I'm scared."

Chapter Four

" "Miss Lyman?"

"Yes." Awakened from a sound sleep, Ilima was still groggy. She squinted at the clock. Only ten o'clock. She'd gone to bed right after dinner and fallen asleep within minutes.

"This is Leilani at Hilo Medical Center. Dr. Kodani asked me to call and tell you that your brother is out of his coma."

"Oh." Sleepiness fled and she sat up in bed fully awake, ready to go. "I'll be right over."

"Please," Leilani hastened to cut in. "Your brother cannot have visitors right now. Dr. Kodani is still in with him, but he asked me to tell you not to come over tonight. Jack has opened his eyes and he's been able to follow movement with them. But

54

he's sleeping right now, a true sleep, and he does need it. If you could just come in the morning as you have been . . . ?'' Her voice trailed off, a question and a suggestion in one.

''Of course.'' Disappointment colored Ilima's voice, but she respected Dr. Kodani and had to conform to his professional opinion. ''I'll be there in the morning.'' She hesitated. ''And thank you for calling.''

''I am sorry that you can't come over right away, but he really is very much better.'' Leilani's care and sympathy communicated itself over the telephone lines.

Ilima thanked her again, then hung up. She left the room, grabbing a lightweight robe that she pulled on as she walked through the house and out to the carport. She knocked at Jack's bedroom door, temporarily Kimo's.

Within seconds, the door was thrown open. Kimo stood there, his eyes dark and somber, his lips pulled into a grim line. He was still dressed in the clothes he'd worn earlier in the day, a paperback novel held open in his hand.

''Did something . . . ?'' The dread was obvious in his voice.

''It's okay,'' Ilima hastened to reassure him. ''I just got a call from Leilani, the intensive care nurse at the hospital. Jack is out of the coma. But she

said not to come over tonight. Dr. Kodani's with
him and he's sleeping right now. A real sleep.''

"Thank goodness.'' Relief flooded through
Kimo like the torrents of water that ran through the
gorge behind their gardens in Maui after a heavy
rain. In his exuberance, he reached for Ilima, en-
closing her in a bear hug. The book fell from his
hand.

He quickly regretted his impulsive action. Ilima
answered in kind, throwing her arms around him to
return the hug. And now he was noticing her in a
whole new way—not as his friend's sister, but as
a warm woman with a body full of soft curves that
molded themselves against his own hard body. She
was tall enough that her head rested comfortably
on his shoulder, and her hair, flying free at this hour
of the night, tickled his nose.

Kimo raised his hand and smoothed the hair
away from his face. It was fine and soft, soft as the
petals of the delicate blossoms she grew. And just
as fragrant. Her hair smelled sweet—a faint and
indescribable scent that reminded him of summer
rain and damp tropical blossoms. And once he'd
touched the silken waves, he found it difficult to
stop. His fingers ran over the strands again and
again as if he were patting a pet kitten.

Finally, Ilima pulled herself away from him,
moving hesitantly, as though uncertain of herself.

"I, uh, guess I'll see you in the morning."

Not waiting for a reply, Ilima turned on her bare-foot heel and dashed across the carport toward the kitchen door.

Inside, Ilima closed the door and stood against it, breathing in deeply and fighting to get control. What had happened? One moment she'd been sharing her good news, and the next she was cradled against Kimo's muscular body, feelings she'd never thought to experience racing through her. She knew he wasn't trying to make a pass. He'd hugged her in the exuberance of the moment, without a thought to the man/woman thing. He was her brother's friend. He probably thought of her as a sister.

Ilima moved away from the door, going to the stove and turning on the burner under the kettle of water. She reached into the cupboard for her tea bags. Chamomile. Yes, that was definitely what she needed. Something relaxing, with health-restoring qualities. She must be ill, because she was suddenly thinking of her brother's friend, the man who was acting like another brother to her, in man/woman terms.

When the tea was ready, Ilima sank into one of the chairs with her hands wrapped around the warm mug. She breathed deep of the herbal scent, hoping the medicinal properties of the drink would cure whatever it was that ailed her. Kimo was her brother's friend, her friend. Nothing more. And she'd better keep reminding herself of that fact.

A quiet tap on the kitchen door startled her into spilling some of the tea in the full mug. It was Kimo, of course. She opened the door.

"I saw the light and thought you might not be able to sleep."

Ilima blushed at the thought of what it was that was keeping her awake. "I, uh, thought some tea would help me settle back down."

"May I join you?"

What could she say? If she told him why she was sitting up drinking herbal concoctions, she'd be too embarrassed ever to look at him again. "Sure." She took another mug from the cupboard. "I didn't know you drank tea."

"I've just acquired a taste for it recently. I had a visitor from England staying with me." He checked his watch for the date. "He left this morning. I was showing him around the business, and we'd have some tea together at the end of the day, talk over what we'd seen and done. I enjoyed it, and the tea was pretty good. It was some type he brought with him from England."

Ilima set the mug of chamomile tea in front of him. "Well, I think this will be a little different. I like herbal teas best myself. No caffeine."

Kimo breathed in the aroma, which seemed to travel on the stream of vapor that moved upward from his mug. "Smells good. Different from the stuff Geoff used."

Kimo moved his gaze from the steaming mug to Ilima's slim frame as she settled back into her chair, pulling her legs up and crossing them on the seat of the chair.

"Actually, Geoff is someone Jack and I met in Africa."

Ilima had had her mug almost to her lips, but now she lowered it to the table. Jack had never mentioned an Englishman. Of course, Jack had never mentioned much of anything about his African experience.

Kimo went on. "Geoff was in the bar that night it was bombed. The place was full of Westerners—that's probably why it was targeted. He wasn't injured, and he helped save a lot of us who were. He helped Jack dig me out and visited us in the hospital afterward."

Ilima filed this away, another bit of information about a trying time in her brother's life. "Was Geoff vacationing on Maui? Didn't Jack want to see him?"

"No to both."

Kimo took a tentative sip of his tea. "A little hot," he told her as he set it back down.

"I told Jack that Geoff was coming. He was here on business, by the way. Jack just told me to say hello for him. Didn't say anything about wanting to see him." Then he smiled. "Geoff has this big old place in England. He says his great-great-great-grandfather—or something like that"—Kimo laughed—"used to raise proteas in his greenhouse. Geoff wants to start up again. That's why he was on Maui—looking over our protea farm. And now he's in New Zealand." He took another look at his watch. "Or on his way there, at any rate."

Ilima listened with interest as he spoke of Geoff. Now that they were together here in the kitchen, she felt more comfortable. It must have been the emotion of the moment that had caused her strange feelings outside his room, because she didn't feel anything more for him now than she had when they were together earlier in the day. Simple affection for a friend who was willing to help her out, to be there for her brother.

Kimo tried another sip of his tea. By now it had cooled enough for a proper taste. "This stuff isn't bad. What is it?"

"Chamomile. It's supposed to be relaxing."

"Well, it's certainly good." He set his mug back on the table and looked earnestly across at Ilima.

"Have you given any more thought to Jack's accident?"

A nervous laugh edging on hysteria escaped from Ilima as she set down her mug. She tried to compose herself with a deep breath.

"It's about all I have thought about." She pushed her hair back from her face. "Not that thinking is accomplishing anything. There just isn't any reason for someone to want to harm Jack."

Kimo nodded. "That's what I think too. None of it makes any sense." He took another drink of tea, taking the time to marshal his thoughts. "I've been reviewing this whole thing ever since we got back here this afternoon. No matter how I try to reconcile it, it just doesn't compute." He shook his head in frustration. "Unless . . ."

Ilima waited, but he didn't continue. His eyes had that unfocused look people got when their minds were busy. Finally, she spoke. "Well, don't just leave it there. Unless what?"

Kimo frowned at her, still mulling over the possibilities. "Well, it sounds like a movie of the week. But the only thing I can think of is that it really *was* an accident, like we originally thought."

"But that doesn't make any sense either," Ilima protested. "Why would someone try to kill him in the hospital if it really was an accident?"

It was obvious that Kimo had given this a great deal of consideration. "I figure it could be two ways. First, maybe that was also an accident. Say the nurse administered the wrong dose or the wrong medication—did they tell you what it was exactly that went wrong?''

Ilima shook her head. "Only that his blood pressure dropped a lot and it was unexpected. The doctor said they were checking on it, and I'm not sure they really knew what had caused it at that point. But something must have made them suspicious enough to call the police. Mostly I was interested in the fact that Jack was okay.''

Kimo took another sip of his tea. His expression was serious. "The second way I figure it is that whoever hit Jack did it accidentally, then panicked and attacked him in the hospital.''

Ilima's eyes widened. Her hands clenched on the warm mug.

Kimo shrugged. "I told you it sounded like a movie of the week.''

"But why would someone take a chance like that if it was an accident? How would they get into the hospital—into intensive care?''

Kimo shrugged again. "Who knows? But people involved in accidents get prosecuted these days. For manslaughter or whatever. And although Jack didn't die immediately, he has been in a coma, so the person might have thought he *would* die. People convicted on manslaughter charges for traffic accidents do go to jail. That could be frightening to someone.''

Ilima nodded. ''Sometimes you hear of famous people—politicians or something—who try to cover up involvement in something like this.'' Ilima's voice was excited, her eyes sparkling with possibilities. Then her eyes moved to Kimo and her demeanor became serious.

''Kimo. Now that Jack's awake . . . I'll understand if you need to return to Maui.'' Her eyes shifted to her hands on the table and she fiddled with the handle of the mug. ''Not that I don't appreciate all you've done to help—''

Kimo interrupted her stammering apology, piercing her with his dark eyes. ''I'm not leaving.'' He realized his voice was harsh and he brought it back to its normal cadence. ''I know you're trying to be considerate and not keep me away from my business for too long. But Geoff's gone now and I haven't had a vacation in a long time. In fact when I told him I was coming here, Dad told me to take as long as I wanted.'' He grinned at her. ''And he's the boss, so you're struck with me for a while longer.'' The grin disappeared. ''Besides, I can't believe you think I would leave with this mystery unresolved.''

Ilima popped up from her chair to press an im-

pulsive kiss on his cheek. "I didn't really want you
to leave," she said, backing away now, embarrassed by her demonstrative display. "But I did feel
obligated to let you know you could." She sank
back into her chair and blessed him with a tender
smile. "I'm glad you're staying."

Kimo returned her smile. It was impossible not
to. He was still feeling shivers down his spine from
that impulsive kiss she'd bestowed on him. "I'm
glad too."

"Let's call Mel tomorrow and tell him your theory about the accident."

Kimo drained his mug and nodded. "Good idea.
Why don't we try to get some sleep now." He
tweaked Ilima under the chin as he gathered up the
mugs and carried them to the sink. "You want to
look well rested and beautiful when you see Jack
tomorrow."

If Ilima had any doubts that Kimo viewed her as
a sister, that small gesture of his laid them to rest.
He probably did the same thing to his three-year-
old niece. She forced a smile. "Are you implying
that I'm not well rested and beautiful now?"

Kimo half turned from the sink where he was
rinsing out the mugs and flashed his smile, the one
that showed his dimple and his straight white teeth.
The one that charmed all the ladies. "Of course

you are. But if you don't get off to bed soon, you might have bags under your eyes. Can't have that.''

"No. Jack wouldn't approve.'' Ilima rose from the table, smiling at Kimo's light, teasing tone.

Kimo finished with his task and wiped off his hands. "Let me leave now and you can be sure the door locks behind me."

"Okay.'' Ilima followed him to the door, stopping with her hand on the knob. How could she have thought there was a sexual attraction between them? He was just a nice guy, taking care of his friend's sister.

"Good night. And Kimo . . .''

Standing in the carport, the dim light casting him in shadow, he turned to look back at her.

Ilima's voice was soft, but carried easily in the still evening air. "*Mahalo* . . . for everything.''

Jack was awake and alert when they reached the hospital the next morning. He lay in his bed, his head propped up on pillows. Ilima rushed into the room, though she stopped short of grabbing him into her arms for a hug and kiss. Instead, she stood beside him, taking his hand in hers while she kissed his sunken cheek. His skin beneath her lips felt dry and scratchy from his need to shave, but it was warm, and his color was an improvement over the last few days.

"Oh, Jack, how *are* you?" Through her tear-damp eyes she could see that his own eyes, so much like her own, were bright.

"Pretty good." His reply sounded hoarse, but there was no mistaking the smile on his lips or the pressure on her hand.

"Hey, brudda." Kimo's greeting was hearty, his smile genuine. "You looking good."

"No need to lie." Jack returned his friend's smile. "I know I'm a mess."

Ilima didn't see the bandage on her brother's head, or the numerous scratches on the side of his face. She didn't notice the scrapes and bruises on his arm or the plaster cast on his leg. All she saw were her brother's eyes, awake and intelligent, and smiling at her.

"You look terrific," she declared. Her voice was low and husky, and she had to clear her throat when she finished speaking. But her smile never wavered, and her eyes glowed with love. For a long moment, she stood beside the bed, holding her brother's hand in hers, content just to stand and look down at him.

Finally, Kimo and Jack together got her to sit in one of the chairs beside the bed. Kimo seated himself beside her so that Jack could talk to both of them comfortably.

"The police were here earlier," Jack told them. "Asking about the accident."

Ilima paled visibly. Her relief at seeing Jack this morning, the fact that he looked so normal . . . It had temporarily pushed the reality of the accident that might not be an accident from her mind.

"What did you tell them about it?"

Jack shook his head, pushing his shoulders up into a shrug at the same time. "I don't remember anything about it. I remember leaving the house for a walk. I took the route I always take, walking up the road toward the mountain. Then the next thing I remember is waking up here last night."

"Did they tell you they're wondering if it really was an accident?" Ilima didn't know whether or not to mention the incident in the hospital, or Dr. Kodani's suspicion of someone tampering with the medication. A quick glance at Kimo supported her decision not to; he gave a short shake of his head, indicating they should keep that quiet for now.

"I figured that was the case. He asked about who might not like me, any enemies, that kind of stuff." Jack's eyes reflected his bafflement at this type of question. "I told them I couldn't think of anybody."

Ilima nodded. "I told him the same thing. Was it Mel Fernandez you talked to? He remembered us from St. Joe."

"Yeah, that's who it was. I remember him." Jack smiled. "I was surprised he remembered me though."

"So was I." Ilima laughed. It was so good to be having this conversation with her brother. He might not remember the accident, but he really was okay. And from what she recalled of Dr. Kodani's earlier conversations with her, some amnesia was not uncommon after a head injury of this kind.

"Looks like you're not going to be taking any late-night walks for a while," Kimo said, indicating the plaster cast that covered Jack's leg from his lower thigh to his ankle.

"Yeah. I wanted to get out of bed this morning, but it's a real project. By the time I got on my feet I was too tired to walk to the john."

Ilima noticed that the sparkle was gone from Jack's eyes. He was such an active person that any inactivity would be hard for him. And as for that cast, he wouldn't be able to do any of his usual work around the gardens with such a large and awkward cast impeding his movements.

"I want to go home, but the doctor said no."

"I should hope so." Ilima burst out with her statement without thinking, then tried to temper it when she saw Jack's disappointment. "I'm sure they have to keep you for a little while, at least. To be sure your head is all right," she added.

Jack looked mollified at her concern for his head injury. But Ilima knew how stubborn he could be, and he'd be badgering the hospital staff about going home for the rest of his time there.

"I do still have a headache," he finally admitted.

Before Ilima could get upset about this admission, or call the nurse for some aspirin, Kimo changed the subject. "Maybe they'll be able to give you a walking cast before you leave," Kimo suggested.

"Hey, that's a great idea."

As the sparkle returned to Jack's eyes, Ilima cast a grateful look to Kimo.

"I'll ask the orthopedist about that," Jack decided. "You wouldn't believe the doctors I've seen since I woke up this morning. But he might have other suggestions to help me get around."

Ilima smiled in delight at the transformation one small suggestion made. She hoped Jack wouldn't be too depressed if the answer to his request for a walking cast was no.

"So . . ." Jack looked between the two of them. "Tell me what I've missed these last couple of days. Did you skip the farmers' market?" He looked at Ilima.

"No, we didn't." She knew he'd be happy at their response. To Jack business was all-important, and he would be glad Kimo had gone for them.

They talked for another half hour before medical personnel arrived and asked them to leave. By then Jack was looking tired enough that Ilima had no objection. She even agreed when Jack suggested that they return to the house until the evening visiting hours.

"I do need some groceries," she said.

"Good. Kimo will take you shopping, won't you, brudda?"

"Sure. You take a long nap. We'll see you later."

Ilima kissed her brother good-bye and edged toward the door. Kimo had to urge her out with a hand at her waist.

"He looks good, doesn't he?" she asked Kimo as soon as they were out of the room.

"Yes, he does."

"I feel so good about Jack, I can hardly stand still."

As though in testimony to her words, she almost bounced across the floor toward the elevators. "Let's hurry with the groceries. I want to get outside and do some real work before it's time to head back here. I need the exercise."

Kimo followed more sedately behind her, his grin wide. His friend was looking pretty good after an accident that could easily have caused his death.

And his friend's sister was smiling and happy—the way a pretty young woman should be.

Kimo decided not to explore his own happiness too deeply. Probably it was caused by his friend's recovery. Yes, that was more than likely the reason. And if not, Kimo wasn't sure he wanted to know the real reason. As he stepped into the elevator with Ilima, it was enough to know that Jack would be all right.

Chapter Five

Ilima hurried in from the kitchen, a can of soda and a glass of ice in her hands. "Here you are. Are you comfortable?" After Jack took them from her hands, she reached for the pillow she'd positioned under his cast, making some adjustment only she could see.

Jack's eyes skittered from his sister over to Kimo. Although Jack's voice remained calm, Kimo felt that his friend was on the edge, ready to rant at his sister for all the solicitous treatment she'd given him since their arrival at the house an hour ago.

Jack had remained in the hospital for only another two days after he awakened from the coma, two days during which he'd swept from acceptance

72

of his new limitations to irritation at being bound to the bed or a wheelchair. Finally, this morning, he'd checked himself out—against doctor's advice. Dr. Kodani had wanted him to stay for another day or two of observation. Head injuries were tricky, he told him, and it was better to be safe. But Jack had had all he could take of lying in bed, letting strangers poke and pry at him. So he'd checked himself out ''ADA.'' Kimo was sure this last fact accounted for much of Ilima's fussiness. She was upset with him for leaving before the doctor gave his okay, but trying hard not to scold him over it— and determined that his health not suffer for it either.

''I'm fine, Ilima. I wish you'd just go on with your day, like I wasn't even here.''

''Sure.'' Ilima nodded absently. Although her answer was what Jack wanted to hear, she continued to glance anxiously his way, examining the area around the sofa to be sure everything he needed was within reach. Although he was far from incapacitated, it was difficult for him to move about with the awkward cast, and she was determined to make things easier for him. In addition to the soda and glass she'd just provided—along with curved drinking straw—there was a crocheted afghan, an extra pillow, and several magazines, all arranged on or under the coffee table in front of the sofa.

The remote for the television lay comfortably at hand, right beside the morning edition of the newspaper. The new crutches he'd use to get around lay on the floor along the front of the couch.

Taking pity on his friend, Kimo approached Ilima and gently turned her toward the door. She'd been up before dawn picking flowers and had barely let up since. He knew she wouldn't agree to taking a nap, but he had to get her away from Jack. "Didn't you tell me there were some flowers ready to mail out? I'll help you package them up."

Ilima allowed herself to be separated from Jack, but reluctantly. "I guess those do have to be mailed. We can't afford to lose any customers." But her gaze trailed back over her shoulder as she left, making eye contact with Jack one last time.

"I guess you should try to take a nap," she suggested to Jack as they left the room.

Kimo's hand exerted a slight pressure on her back, urging her out of the room quickly. He hoped she didn't hear Jack's muttering. He couldn't make out the words, but he had a pretty good idea of what they were, and he didn't think they were anything Ilima should hear. Jack definitely needed a little time away from his sister.

Ilima continued to be distracted as she and Kimo crossed the driveway to the large shed the Lymans used as a workroom. Her mind was still with Jack and his problems.

She managed to pull herself back to the present as they reached the shed door. A one-room building, the shed had been little more than a roof set on posts when their grandmother was alive. It was one of the first improvements she and Jack had made to the business, closing it off into a workable space they could use no matter the weather. Now it was a large, airy room, lined with jalousied windows. Shelves for supplies filled the space beneath the windows, and a large worktable stood in the center of the room.

Kimo opened the door, stepping aside to allow Ilima to enter first.

"Will you be doing the farmers' market again tomorrow?" Ilima asked.

"I wasn't planning on it. I thought you would be going, now that Jack's out of the hospital."

Ilima's eyes were troubled. "I can't leave him."

"I'd be here with him."

Kimo could see Ilima struggling with the idea of going on with business as usual—if it meant leaving the property and Jack. She chewed on her lower lip, and her hands were clumsy when she reached for the boxes she needed. He took the flattened boxes from her hands and quickly set them up.

Buckets of cut flowers, leaves, and ferns sat on the floor beside the worktable.

"Thank you." She took the boxes absently, giving an automatic response. The red anthuriums lay closest beside her, and she took the flowers from the bucket and laid them on the work surface.

"I know he'd be all right with you, Kimo. It's just so hard for me to leave him. I keep thinking, what if something else happens? If I'm here at least I have a chance of helping." She started laying the small squares of slit paper over the spadices of the anthuriums, and the familiar pattern of the work was calming.

"You have to be realistic about this, Ilima." Kimo lined the boxes with long green ti leaves as he spoke. "You have a business to run, and you're going to be one person short for a while. Even when Jack gets a walking cast on his leg, he's going to be limited in what he can do. You can't just sit here with him all the time."

He finished lining the boxes and began to wrap the heliconia blooms in paper to protect them in transit. He continued to talk as his fingers did the work.

"As for someone coming after him . . . It's hard to imagine. But just what will you do? Call nine-one-one? Jack can handle that himself. You're a strong capable person, Ilima, but face it." Kimo stopped working temporarily while he made his point. "If a man comes in here meaning to harm Jack, you won't be able to do much. Feminism aside, women are just smaller and weaker than most men."

Ilima was listening, but her lips had tightened into a grim line, and he could almost see the steam venting from her ears. He went back to work on the flowers but looked over at her with a wry smile. "Besides, Jack has only been home for an hour and he's already going nuts with all the attention you're giving him."

Ilima's eyes grew wide and her hands stilled. Mention of Jack's attitude had effectively drained her anger; all her thoughts right now centered on her concern for her brother.

"Oh, no, I don't think so." But her voice trailed off as she thought about Jack's attitude for the last few minutes they were in the house. He *had* seemed a little agitated. With a start, she realized that Kimo might be right. "Well, maybe a little. But he does need someone to get things for him. That cast is heavy and awkward."

Her eyes lit up as a new thought came to her. "And he can't carry things and work the crutches at the same time. Besides," she added, "he's still very weak."

"I know that, and you know that. But I don't

think Jack is willing to admit it.'' Kimo had started on the bird of paradise, carefully wrapping each of the large orange-and-blue blossoms. ''You're going to have to lighten up, Ilima, or Jack is going to explode.''

Ilima put down the stem she held, and clutched the edge of the table. Grabbing on to something hard seemed to help release some of the frustration she felt about Jack's accident and its aftermath. ''I'll try, Kimo. But it's not easy.''

To her embarrassment, her voice caught at the end of the statement. She tried to continue with the next anthurium. But her eyesight had gone cloudy as her eyes dampened, and her fingers slid past the stem of the flower without grasping it. Her voice was soft and thready when she spoke again. ''I don't want anything more to happen to Jack.''

Kimo watched Ilima's hands as she fumbled with the flowers. She was hurting and he knew it. But could he trust himself to take her into his arms, to comfort her? The last time he had done it, he'd found himself recognizing her as more than his friend's sister. And the thought still scared him.

''I know. I don't want him hurt any more either.''

He saw her blink rapidly, and his heart turned over. Without further thought of reactions or consequences, Kimo reached for Ilima and gathered her into his arms. Her head lay comfortably on his shoulder, and he stroked her hair in a gentling motion. He loved the feel of her hair, as soft as the folds of a silk scarf. His other hand slid over her back, rubbing some of the tension from her body.

To his relief, she began to relax. If she shed any tears, he didn't notice them. Her arms came up to encircle his waist, and Kimo lost all consciousness of real time. Her body was soft and curved and fit beautifully against his own hard one. A subtle fragrance, reminiscent of tropical rain showers, came from her hair. He breathed deeply of the scent, so fresh and clean, and thought of his home in the Maui mountains. Rain showers were frequent there, much more so than here in Puna. He loved the way the earth smelled just before and at the start of the rain; it was a scent forever tied to his image of home and family, one that left him with a comfortable feeling of all's-right-with-the-world. Somehow her hair seemed to hold that same wonderful scent, a scent that was released each time he touched it. No wonder he never tired of running his fingers over her hair.

Ilima felt the soft fabric of Kimo's well-worn T-shirt against her cheek, and closed her eyes. He smelled of soap—a clean, refreshing scent with a citrus base. It was the same soap she had in the kitchen, the one she used to wash her hands. Yet it had never smelled quite like this—like lime and mint and clean male. Would she ever be able to wash her hands again without remembering this tender moment?

She moved her head and her cheek rubbed against the soft cotton of his shirt. The thump of his heartbeat reverberated in her ear, slow and steady—comforting. His was not the body of a male model, although he was athletic and muscular. Kimo was built like the warriors of their ancestors, tall and broad. Yet his solid bulk was comforting to her. It was amazing what solace could be found in the warmth of a human touch. Perhaps it was just the feeling that you were no longer alone.

With this thought in mind, Ilima felt herself relax in Kimo's embrace. Of course, she was also grateful to him for his steadying presence this past week. And now, the pressure of having Jack home—without his doctor's permission—of trying to care for him and protect him . . . It was all creating more stress in her life than she felt ready to cope with. She and Jack had been caring for each other all their lives; but this time, with unknown threats hovering in the background, she just wasn't sure she would be able to protect her brother. But at this moment, with Kimo warm and solid in her arms, she felt ready to face anything—and overcome it.

Yes. Undoubtedly, these were the reasons she felt that odd flutter in her tummy when Kimo held her, that strange increase in blood flow that made her hands and feet feel so warm.

Beginning to feel a hum along her nerve endings, Ilima gave Kimo a hug, then pulled back enough to look up into his face.

"You're pretty special, you know that?"

Kimo stared down into Ilima's pale eyes. He was fascinated by those cider-colored eyes she shared with her twin brother. Yet he would never mistake her eyes for Jack's. He'd heard it said that the eyes were the reflection of the soul, and in Ilima's case he thought it must be true. Her beauty came out in her eyes. Right now he could see that she was happy. He could see her gratitude. . . .

He didn't want gratitude from Ilima. He'd only done what he considered to be right, coming as soon as he heard about his friend's accident. It was the Hawaiian way to help those who needed help. And Ilima and Jack had needed help. He hadn't done anything extraordinary. And what he wanted from Ilima right now had nothing to do with gratitude.

Keeping his eyes on hers, Kimo lowered his head and touched his lips to hers.

That first touch, light and gentle though it was,

was as sharp as an electric shock for both of them. It was enough of a surprise that Kimo almost stopped, almost pulled back in alarm. Almost.

Ilima had seen Kimo lowering his head. She'd seen the soft look in his eyes, the sparkle that heralded an action ready to be taken. She wasn't surprised that he kissed her. But the shock of that first touch of their lips—that was a surprise. A wonder. A marvel.

Words finally deserted her as the pressure of his lips increased. Feeling took over. A warm sense of comfort spread through her, and her arms crept up around his shoulders. Her fingers touched the nape of his neck and traveled up into the locks of hair that curled above his collar.

Kimo felt the touch of her hands on his nape all the way down to his toes. Trying to repress a shiver of pleasure, he ended the kiss. With a feeling of extreme reluctance, he eased back, widening the space between them. Ilima looked up at him, a dazed look in her eyes, her lips softly parted.

With a reluctant sigh, he released her from his embrace and took a small step back. She looked so beautiful at that moment, her eyes all soft with feeling, her lips pink from his kiss. He wanted to take her back into his arms; he wanted to kiss her again and never stop.

Once again, Kimo looked into her light brown

eyes and was almost lost. He didn't know if he could control himself unless he put immediate distance between them. Reminding himself that this was his best friend's sister, he took another step back.

"I, uh, think I'd better go start dinner."

Ilima blinked after him as he immediately turned and hurried from the shed. Start dinner? They'd just had lunch! Her heart sank as she realized he was just making an excuse to get away from her. Apparently their kiss hadn't been as special for him as it had been for her. She'd never felt anything like it before.

Dazed and confused, Ilima watched him go. Feeling deserted, she returned to packaging the flowers, dividing the wrapped blossoms among the prepared boxes. But the mechanical movements of the process couldn't keep her mind engaged and off of Kimo.

By the time the boxes of flowers were ready, Ilima had come to the conclusion that she cared more for Kimo than was wise. The man was tall, attractive—infinitely desirable to any woman. Women who were beautiful, who had interesting and exciting jobs, would fall all over themselves for someone like Kimo. How could she possibly compete?

As she loaded the boxes into the truck, she

scolded herself for entertaining any schoolgirl fantasies about her brother's friend. He was from another island, for goodness' sake. Another island where he had a large family and a share in their business. Now that Jack was home, he'd be returning to Maui soon. And her life would go on, here, in Puna. She and Jack had a family business to maintain too, and they had only themselves to run it.

No, there was no future for her with Kimo. Only infinite heartache.

Chapter Six

Ilima pulled into the driveway, tired after the long morning in downtown Hilo. Business at the farmers' market had been good; the morning was sunny and warm, both tourists and serious shoppers plentiful. Yet her mind had been troubled. She worried about Jack and how he was coping. Thoughts of the accident that might not be accidental still had her in a turmoil. And despite her resolution of the previous day, thoughts of Kimo flashed through her mind at odd moments. Her previously ordered world was in a jumble, and events no longer followed sensible patterns.

As she climbed out of the truck, she noted that their old Ford Escort was gone. Kimo was probably making another run to the supermarket in Keaau.

Despite her worries, she couldn't suppress a grin. She and Jack hadn't eaten so well since their grandmother passed away.

Thoughts of Kimo filled her mind as she unloaded the truck and rinsed out buckets. His kindness, his good looks, his irrepressible spirit—all were part of the package that made up Kimo Ahuna. He was a pretty special person. She just wished she could eliminate all memories of that kiss they'd shared.

Well, maybe not *all*.

Ilima quickly turned the dreamy smile that memory spawned into a rigid frown. She had to relegate Kimo to his role as family friend. Anything else would mean nothing but misery for her, and eventually for all of them—herself, Kimo, and even Jack.

She'd just made this decision when the Ford turned up the drive, and Kimo parked the small car beside the truck. Watching him remove his large frame from the compact car reminded her of circus acts and clowns, and brought a smile to her lips. Jack sat in the passenger seat beside Kimo, and was having his own problems removing himself and his cast from the small car. But he motioned Ilima away when she tried to help him.

Kimo greeted her warmly, making a few comments about traffic. ''I needed a few things at the store and thought Jack might enjoy getting out. I thought sure we'd beat you home." The two men exchanged a guilty look, and Ilima realized she wouldn't have heard about Jack's excursion at all if they hadn't been caught up in traffic.

Trying not to overreact, Ilima asked Jack how he'd managed.

"Oh, it was great. I'm getting pretty good with these things now," he said, gesturing with one of the crutches and almost knocking himself over. He quickly caught himself on the door of the car, correcting his balance and putting the two crutches in place under his arms.

Biting her lip to control her tongue, Ilima finished unloading the truck. Why didn't Jack realize he should be resting? He needed to get his strength back after the trauma he'd suffered, and he needed time for his leg to heal.

Kimo watched Ilima, his eyes dancing with merriment. She was so mad at him for taking Jack shopping, she would probably enjoy throwing one of her buckets at his head. One filled with water. He knew better than to laugh out loud, though. Instead he hauled a number of filled plastic grocery sacks from the backseat and headed into the house, calling after Jack to hurry.

Ilima bundled the last of the unsold flowers into a bucket of water and stamped off toward the shed with it. She was trying so hard not to hover over Jack, and Kimo was goading him on. She couldn't bear to watch as Jack worked his way slowly toward the house. If only she had a wheelchair to help him . . . But no, Jack would never have allowed it.

She bit her lip as she washed up, taking several deep breaths for good measure. Then she headed for the house.

Ilima entered by the front door, avoiding the kitchen Kimo had entered a short time before. She rationalized that she needed to check on Jack. She and Kimo had insisted that he move back into his old bedroom for the time being. With a laugh, Kimo claimed squatting rights to Jack's new room. What none of them said, but all three understood, was that Jack would not be able to manage on his own in the room off the carport with its tiny bathroom. Until the cast came off, or was cut down considerably, he'd have to stay in the main house, where the rooms were larger, and there was more space for him to maneuver with the ungainly cast.

Much as she loved her brother, Ilima had to admit that he was very difficult to live with at the moment. He was chafing at the necessary confinement, and his temper was getting ragged, but Ilima was still finding it difficult not to fuss over him. Perhaps the trip to the store with Kimo had been just the thing, after all. She'd expected him to be in his room, worn out from his first expedition. Instead, he was seated on the couch, anxious to see her. He wanted to hear all about the market, about what sold and what didn't, and what the other flower sellers had brought with them.

Ilima told him everything she could remember about her morning. Kimo, banging around in the kitchen, stuck his head in the door periodically to add his comments. Jack and Ilima had just joined him in the kitchen when the doorbell rang.

Peering through the glass insert in the front door, Ilima was surprised to see Mel Fernandez. Surprised, but delighted. Maybe he'd determined what had happened that night at the hospital, and had come with good news. She threw open the door.

"Mel. Come on in." She stood back from the doorway, making room for Mel to step inside. "Kimo just got back from the grocery store and made some sandwiches for lunch. Why don't you join us?"

"Well, if it's no imposition." Mel followed Ilima into the kitchen, where Jack sat at the table and Kimo stood at the counter. He nodded a greeting to Kimo before approaching Jack.

"How are you, Jack? You're looking much better."

Jack gave a short bark of laughter. "I guess. But I'm itching to get out and actually do some work."

"He's going stir-crazy." Ilima came over to the table, her arms full of soft drink cans. She set them in the center of the table and went back to the cupboard for glasses. "But he can't do much until that cast comes off."

Kimo joined them at the table as Ilima finished setting out the plates. "Here you are. This will make you feel better." He put a large platter of sandwiches in the center of the table and sat down, eagerly taking one of the sandwiches for his own plate. "I made turkey, ham, and corned beef. Help yourself."

Ilima passed a bowl of potato chips and unscrewed the top from a jar of pickles. "Have you found out anything more about the accident?" she asked Mel.

Mel put down untouched the sandwich he'd had halfway to his mouth. "Actually, we have made some progress with the accident."

Movement around the table stilled as the others became immediately attentive.

"Nothing that can help us identify the person who hit you." Mel cast an apologetic look toward Ilima, who had released a sigh of disappointment at this news. "However, combing the accident area, we did find some bits of glass that came from the headlight of a Dodge van. There were some bits in your clothing too.'' Mel nodded at Jack. ''Almost microscopic bits actually, but that's how we know the glass is from this accident and not something that happened a week before.''

Kimo grinned. ''That's pretty good police work.''

''There was one other thing.'' Mel looked at Jack. ''Your watch.''

''Your watch?'' Ilima glanced down at her brother's bare left arm, suddenly realizing that Jack hadn't been wearing his watch since he returned home from the hospital. His left wrist showed a pale stripe of skin where his watch usually encircled it.

Jack followed Ilima's gaze to his wrist. ''I found my watch in the nightstand at the hospital. I gave it to Mel that day we talked. The crystal broke when I was hit. And there was paint on the watchband.''

Mel nodded again. ''You were right about the paint being from the car that hit you. That particular beige paint was used on Dodge vans for several years. We're waiting to hear if the lab can give us a particular year, using the paint and glass samples.''

"Wow. I'm impressed." Ilima put a pickle slice in her turkey sandwich, carefully replacing the bread. "It sounds just like a TV show."

Mel winced. "I hope not. Most of those shows are a lot of fiction."

"Hey, come on. Too much talking, not enough eating." Kimo waved at the food sitting mostly untouched on the table.

The kitchen was quiet for a while after that, with only the natural sounds of food being passed and eaten. Noisy mynah birds chattered outside the windows, and traffic noises from the highway drifted in with the breeze. A few comments passed back and forth on popular television shows, moving on to a recent movie.

Then the sandwiches were gone and they were sitting around the table finishing their soft drinks. Kimo brought out some chocolate chip cookies he'd purchased at the store's bakery. Mel returned to business.

"So, Jack . . . I take it you haven't remembered anything more about the night of the accident."

Jack shook his head. "I remember going out for a walk. I walk the same route when I go out every night. Down the street here, then I turn right and head up the side road. Sometimes I go through the gardens until I come out up there. Then I walk up through the side streets in that area, depending on how long I want to stay out. There are a lot of small streets, and not all the lots are developed. I do remember doing that, taking my long route, then coming back down here to the highway. But that's it. Nothing after that.'' He shook his head again. ''And, man, I've tried. I feel like my brain is being wrung out, but absolutely nothing about that will come back. I've even tried to imagine lights coming at me. . . .'' His eyes took on a glazed expression as he pictured what he imagined the scene to be. ''But, still, nothing.''

Mel put his half-eaten cookie down and was shaking his head. ''There wouldn't have been lights coming at you. You were hit from behind.''

Jack and Ilima both stared. Neither of them had thought to question just exactly how the accident had occurred. And Kimo kicked himself for not inquiring about this when he'd first spoken to Mel after the incident at the hospital.

Ilima returned to her brother's last comment, frowning at him as she spoke. ''I thought Dr. Kodani told you not to force it. That your memory will come back on its own, when it's time.''

Jack's mouth turned down in angry frustration. He pushed away his plate, his dessert untasted. ''That's easy for him to say. He doesn't have this empty black spot hanging over him, with an accident that might not have been an accident. And no logical reason to explain anything other than an accidental hit-and-run.''

Ilima rose from her chair and hurried to stand behind her brother, putting her hands on his shoulders. ''Oh, Jack.''

It was the wrong thing to do. Still angry at his inability to do much or to remember anything, Jack brushed her hands from his shoulders. Ilima's eyes clouded with hurt and she blinked rapidly a few times. But she moved away from him, busying herself by clearing the table.

Kimo sent his friend a quick disappointed look and rose to help Ilima. A soft touch on the arm when they met at the sink, a gentle stroke on the shoulder as they reached across the table for the last of the dishes . . . Kimo hoped these small contacts would show Ilima his support and help her handle the rejection from her twin. But she shied from his touch in much the same way she'd twisted away from Jack's rough dismissal.

Ilima was trying to concentrate on cleaning up. It would be easier if Kimo would just sit back down and visit with the other two men. She was having enough trouble coping with Jack's treatment of her. She didn't need Kimo trying so hard to be understanding. She didn't need his close physical contact.

She blinked back the moisture dampening her

eyes. It felt too good, his quiet support. And she was afraid to become dependent on it. It was important that they remain just friends.

How could Jack treat her this way? Of course she knew how hard it was for him—not knowing about the accident and its causes. It was hard on all of them. But most of all, she realized that the enforced inaction was driving Jack crazy. She knew that was what fueled his anger, caused him to snap at her for small things, and caused the rejection just now when all she'd wanted to do was to comfort him.

But still, it was hard to take. And he'd only been home for twenty-four hours. What would he be like after a week? Or two weeks? The large cast would probably be on his leg for a month; after that the doctor said he would get a smaller one. But that one would be needed for a month or two as well. The orthopedist had not been too precise with times, claiming the need for examinations and X rays before making those decisions. Now she wondered if he'd already noticed the trapped look in Jack's eyes and had been trying to keep him from getting depressed. If that was the case, it didn't seem to be working.

Kimo watched Ilima finish putting the leftovers into the refrigerator. He'd given up, joining the men back at the table, leaving her to handle the cleanup tasks. She needed the physical activity to help her handle Jack's frustrated rejection of her.

He understood what was happening with his friend, but he didn't have to like it. He was going to have a few words with Jack later. But for now he sat, watching Ilima and listening to Mel question Jack once again about possible enemies from his past.

When Ilima returned to her seat, Kimo reached for her hand. He held it briefly, giving it a gentle squeeze before releasing it again. Her eyes sought his, but instead of the soft smile he'd hoped to see, her gaze remained distant, her lips pulled tight. Then, as though she realized that he really wanted only to help, her lips tipped upward into a brief smile.

Kimo felt that smile right down into his heart—a brief tightness in his chest coupled with a momentary inability to catch his breath. Confused by this physical reaction to Ilima's brief attention, Kimo was temporarily distracted. By the time he brought himself back to the present, everyone was rising and Mel was issuing his thanks for the luncheon. They all moved into the front room, Jack muttering to himself as he handled the crutches with little grace.

Mel issued some warnings about being careful

and locking the doors. Then, asking them to call him with any further news or ideas, he left.

Ilima had reason to remember Mel's leave-taking and his warnings later that day. She spent the afternoon working with the *Heliconia psittacorums,* removing dead leaves and applying fertilizer. Some of the clumps had finished flowering and needed to be cut to the ground to encourage new growth. She and Jack had been adding more varieties of the parrot's-beak heliconias, and they now were an important part of their business. Small but showy, the parrot's-beak heliconias, came in numerous varieties, from rosy yellow to deep red to many shades of orange. She'd spent the afternoon among the "Sassy" heliconias, those bright red-orange flowers rising from the apple green bracts. On Monday she would continue her work among the more yellow "Parrot" hybrids. Exotic and beautiful, yet still small in size, the parrot's-beak heliconias were an ideal flower for shipping to the mainland. The cut flowers could last two to three weeks and were rapidly becoming as popular as the heart-shaped anthuriums.

Tired and dirty from her afternoon of gardening, Ilima moved toward the house, anxious for a hot shower. Her mind was still on the beds of heliconias, running through the report she would share with Jack of all she'd done and all that still needed doing. It made him feel a part of things if he could hear about her activity in detail, and she was anxious to oblige.

As she came out of the garden near the shed, she saw a tall but scrawny young man dressed in shorts and a T-shirt standing near the corner of the house. Surprised, she stopped for a moment, standing still as she stared. He appeared to be peering into the window. *Her* window!

"Hey!" Ilima's hand clenched on the handle of the spade she still held. Without thinking, she ran forward, shouting at the intruder. "What are you doing?"

Her shout startled the trespasser, sending him dashing toward the street. Ilima had always considered herself a fast runner. She'd done some running in high school, and still did some occasional jogging. But this young man was *fast*. By the time she got around the house and down the driveway, he was climbing into a beige van that was pulled over on the shoulder of the highway in front of their house. Someone must have been waiting inside, with the engine running. Before the man had even shut the door fully, the van was pulling out into traffic, causing a lot of horn-blowing and nasty hand signals from those already on the highway.

Within moments it had sped away, lost in the distance among all the other cars.

Ilima stood in the driveway, sweaty, dirty, and now breathing hard. Her heart was beating at double its normal rate, and not solely because of her race around the house. What was going on here? Had he been looking for Jack?

Kimo ran up behind her, his feet bare in the dust of the drive. A quick glance back showed her that Jack was standing in the doorway, the crutches under his arms. He was looking at the ground outside the front door, speculation in his eyes. Ilima rushed back toward the house before he could join them in the yard. He might be getting good at managing the crutches, but she didn't want to see him walking with them on the rough ground outdoors.

"Did you see that?" Ilima was almost shouting in her excitement as she hurried back toward the house. "A beige van." She stopped beside her brother, her eyes sparkling with energy. "Jack! Did you see it?"

At her hurried approach, Jack had stopped on the front landing. Now he stared down the highway in the direction the van had taken. Ilima couldn't tell if he even heard her. Unblinking, his eyes remained concentrated on a spot in the distance.

But Kimo was listening. And anxious. "We heard you shout. What happened?"

In her rush to prevent Jack's leaving the smooth concrete at the front of the house, Ilima had almost forgotten that Kimo had rushed out after her. He hadn't even taken the time to put on a pair of rubber slippers; he'd just run out in his bare feet.

Ilima took a deep breath. Her breathing was back to normal but her heart still pounded its too-rapid beat. ''I was coming in to clean up before dinner. And there was this guy standing at the back of the house. He was peering in my bedroom window.''

Kimo took her shoulders in his hands. ''And you shouted at him? You *chased* him?'' Kimo's voice was rising as he spoke. ''Are you nuts?'' He was so agitated, he gave her a little shake.

Ilima twisted out of his hold. ''I just reacted. What would you do if you saw someone staring in your window?''

Kimo didn't know the answer to that, but he did know that he didn't like her response. He ran his eyes over her, checking to be sure that she was all right. She wore her usual work outfit of worn jeans and an old shirt. The legs of her jeans were smeared with mud and dirt, her hair falling out of the ponytail she'd pulled it into. There was a smudge on her right cheekbone. Her head was held high and her pale eyes sparkled with indignation. Still gripped in her hand was a small spade. She looked like an *ali'i* chieftainess, ready to do battle. She looked beautiful. Best of all, she looked okay.

And at the moment she was regarding Jack in an odd way. Kimo turned his attention to his friend. Jack was still staring up the highway, his eyes unblinking and unfocused, his brow furrowed.

Kimo shook his head, wondering if that head wound had caused more damage than the doctor realized. Didn't Jack realize that his sister had been in danger?

"We have to go in and call Mel, Jack." Ilima managed to turn her brother around and pushed him inside. "That was a beige van, and I'll bet anything it had a smashed headlight."

"But that's the thing," Kimo insisted, following them into the house. "You shouldn't have run after him. What if he'd turned and attacked you? We know these guys are dangerous, and we still don't know why."

Ilima turned an exasperated look toward Kimo. "And how was I to know he was driving a beige van when I just saw him all alone in back of the house?" She dialed the phone as she spoke. "He looked like some high school punk trying to break into the house."

Jack had returned to his usual place on the sofa. His expression still put him far from the scene. And he had yet to say a word.

Kimo moved over to the chair where he often sat and played card games with Jack. Jack didn't seem to notice.

Kimo decided to wait. By the time Ilima joined them, Jack had pulled himself out of the trancelike state he'd been in. He blinked at Ilima, then at Kimo. ''I've seen that van before.''

Ilima clutched her hands together to contain her excitement. Maybe this was the end of this nightmare. Without realizing it, she reached out to take Kimo's hand, squeezing it hard. Her eyes remained fixed on Jack's face.

Jack made a fist and brought it down hard against the arm of the sofa. The thump seemed loud in the small room, and caused his sister to jump. ''For all the good it does. The only thing I remember about it is that I've seen it before. When I take those long walks at night . . . There's not a lot of traffic at that time of night. But I often see a beige van like that one on the road.''

''That's it?'' Kimo couldn't help but sound annoyed that the great revelation revealed so little. He was aware, however, that Ilima had taken his hand in her excitement, and that she still held on to it.

Jack pounded his fist against the sofa arm once more. This time the action and the noise did not startle anyone. ''Darn, but I wish it was more than that.'' He pushed his hand through his hair, making the brown strands stand up in disarray. "But that's it. That's all I remember. I don't think there's anything else, but I don't know. And none of it makes any sense."

As they pondered this new information, the phone rang. It was Mel returning their call. Jack and Ilima shared the phone, going over the new information with him.

"Someone will be out first thing in the morning to see about lifting tire prints from the side of the road where the van was parked," Mel told them. "It might be too late by then, but it's too dark now."

Ilima was surprised to see that it had indeed grown dark while they talked.

"We get up early. Just tell them to come to the door and we'll show them where it was parked."

Kimo watched in silence while the twins spoke to Mel, taking turns on the phone. He'd thought he would be back on Maui by now. But how could he leave with all that was happening? He'd spent most of the week worrying about his old friend Jack. Today, it had come as a surprise how intense his feelings were when he'd feared for Ilima. Her shout had startled the two men, then galvanized them into action. He could still feel the relief that had flooded him when he'd seen Ilima panting in the driveway and realized that she was unharmed. He'd wanted to chase that van himself and get that kid before he had a chance to harm Ilima or Jack, or even just to upset them again.

Ilima finished her conversation with Mel and pressed the button to disconnect the cordless phone. She sat on the couch beside Jack, the two of them communing silently for a few minutes in the unique way that twins could. Finally she squeezed Jack's hand and got up.

''I'm so dirty.'' She looked down at her grubby clothes with a sigh. ''I need to clean up. Mel said to be sure everything is locked up. . . .''

She moved tiredly toward the front door to re-check that they'd locked it, then started for the kitchen. Kimo stopped her.

''You need a good soak. Make the water nice and hot and lie back and relax.'' He turned her toward the bathroom and urged her forward with his fingers between her shoulder blades. ''I'll make sure the back door is locked when I get out to the kitchen. I have to check on the stew I started for dinner anyway.''

Ilima started to protest, but then gave up. She was too tired. And he was right. He was heading that way anyhow. It was such a relief to listen to his instructions and head for a hot tub that Ilima completely forgot how much she hated taking orders from anyone—especially a man.

Chapter Seven

Despite the excitement of the previous day, Ilima, Jack, and Kimo spent a quiet Sunday together. Ilima awoke early as promised, showing the two men from the police department where they'd seen the van the previous evening. But Kimo and Jack were also up and about and not willing to be excluded. They insisted on helping, which meant it took almost half an hour for them all to agree on the exact location where the van had been parked.

It turned out to be an act of frustration anyway. It had been dry for the last few days, and the ground along the shoulder was too hard. There were no tire prints to be found.

Afterward, Ilima decided to attend morning

mass, something she had done sporadically in recent years but wanted to do this morning.

"I feel I have to go in and give thanks," she told Kimo while Jack was still in the other room.

He nodded his understanding. He kept his voice low, not wanting Jack to overhear. "I'd go with you, but I don't want to leave Jack alone." Unsaid in the air between them: *Especially after our visitor yesterday.*

The three of them had spent hours the night before discussing the day's events. Although they all wanted to believe it was just a juvenile delinquent looking for a quick way to earn a few dollars, the accident hung over them—the accident and its aftermath. No one even wanted to state out loud that the incident in the hospital might have been attempted murder.

Then there was the beige van that had driven off with the interloper—how could that be a coincidence?

Ilima didn't know how the men felt, but she had gone to bed exhausted. It wasn't just that she'd worked hard physically that day; it was the emotional upheaval of her world. She'd thought everything would be all right now that Jack was home and recovering nicely. How naive she'd been to think everything would return to normal. That kid peering in the window—*her* window—was not something she would soon forget. And the thought that it was connected with Jack's accident would not go away.

But at least she'd slept well—once she'd fallen asleep.

So on that Sunday morning Ilima found a particular comfort in the familiar prayers and songs of the Catholic service. Afterward, feeling refreshed and more optimistic than she had in days, she stopped at the bakery for fresh pastries, and rented an action thriller for them to watch. All she wanted was to spend a quiet day relaxing with her brother and Kimo. A hot cup of lemon and honey tea and some still-warm *malasadas,* the Sunday comics . . . What more could a gal want?

Kimo strolled into the room and sat on the floor beside her. Ilima stifled the impulse to answer her own rhetorical question. Of course a gal could want a man. A tall, charming man with a gentle, caring nature and no fear of hard work.

"So, how's it going?"

Ilima smiled at him. "No complaints." She lowered her voice so that Jack wouldn't hear her. "Thanks for staying with Jack so I could go to church this morning. I wouldn't have felt comfortable leaving him here alone."

She laid the paper flat on the floor before her and picked up her mug, wrapping both hands around it.

Not that she needed to warm herself when Kimo was in the room. On the contrary, just having him near made her feel the need to open a window in search of a cooling breeze. But she felt an insane impulse to take and hold his hand; better to warm her hands with her tea mug.

Kimo shrugged his shoulders in a natural gesture that said it all. It was nothing. It was something he would do for any friend.

Because his physical presence was so large, when Kimo shrugged, his shoulders brushed against Ilima's. She had a reaction so sharp it caused a small shudder throughout her body that she managed to camouflage by moving quickly to set aside her tea and reach once more for the paper.

''I'm glad you're here to help Jack with the shower.''

Although she folded the small section of the newspaper and set it on her lap, she didn't look at it.

Kimo laughed. ''Yeah. It would be hard for you to help him stumble in and out of there, all right.''

Kimo tried to laugh and be casual. It was one of the hardest things he'd ever done. When he entered the room, it had just seemed natural to join her on the floor. She sat there with the Sunday paper spread out all around her, bent over the funnies like a young girl. She'd changed out of the dress she wore to church into a pair of faded shorts, and her bare knees were nicely rounded, with a length of shapely brown leg showing below them. Since the newspaper took up so much of the floor space, he'd squeezed into the small spot of bare carpet just beside her. Bad idea. His knee brushed hers as he sat, trying to compress his large body into as small an area as possible. Heat surged upward from the spot where they'd touched, making him even more aware of her.

Ilima had reacted quickly also, pulling her knees in, away from him. But then he'd been foolish enough to shrug. It was a gesture he used a lot, one he'd been trying to curb. If only he'd done so this time! The feel of her soft shoulder against his— even though his arm was covered with a T-shirt— was enough to heat him even more.

When Ilima offered him the page of comics she'd already read, he grabbed at them, levering himself up and onto the sofa. Jack wouldn't be in for another few minutes. Heck, the guy could prop his leg on the coffee table rather than stretch it across the length of the couch. He was going to sit here for now, and not get up until Ilima either left the room or turned back into the shy and awkward girl that he remembered from previous visits.

He shook out the paper and held it up in front of him. Then, unable to resist, he lowered it enough to glance over the top at Ilima. Her hair was down this morning, flowing over her shoulders in a glorious riot of dark waves—not black, not brown, but some wonderful combination of the two. Red-gold streaks colored the top layer of her hair where the sun had lightened it, giving the whole a radiance that shone in the bright morning light that poured in the front windows. Her knit top left most of her shoulders bare so that her golden brown skin glowed in the honeyed light. Although her legs were folded up and back in her position on the floor, he could see that they were perfection itself.

Nope, no chance of ever again looking upon her as a sister. He had sisters. None of them brought about the kind of feelings in him that Ilima did when he just looked upon her.

Kimo was still sitting behind the newspaper surreptitiously studying Ilima when Jack stumped into the room. His crutches made a distinctive noise on the wood floor in the hall, then became muffled as he moved into the carpeted living room.

"Man, I'll be glad to get rid of these things."

Ilima bounced up like a child's jack-in-the-box as Jack seated himself on the sofa. "Shall I get you something?"

Jack frowned at her. "I hate having you wait on me like this, Ilima."

"It's hard for you to carry things with the

crutches, though I notice that you're getting much better at using them.'' She smiled as she offered the compliment. ''And I know you'd do the same for me if I hurt my leg.''

Jack reluctantly agreed. ''I guess a soda would taste good.''

Ilima left immediately for the kitchen.

Jack looked over at Kimo, still sitting on the opposite side of the sofa studying the colorful sheet of comics.

''Okay. Spill it.''

Kimo lowered the paper but didn't say anything. He raised one eyebrow in a silent question.

''I can tell something's going on here.''

Suddenly a slow grin appeared and grew, transforming Jack's face, erasing the lines of pain and doubt that had lately marked it. He looked ten years younger.

''It's you and Ilima, isn't it?'' He reached over to slap Kimo on the shoulder. ''Man, this is great. I've been hoping she would meet someone nice. But you!'' He laughed again. ''I don't know why I didn't think of it. It's perfect.''

Kimo was staring at him in disbelief, but Jack didn't notice.

''It's almost worth the accident to have you and Ilima find each other.''

Ilima walked in the door with the can of soda in

one hand, a plate of *malasadas* in the other—just in time to hear Jack's last line. Her eyebrows shot upward and she almost spilled the plate of pastries, righting the dish just before the round doughnuts slid off the edge.

"What—?"

"We didn't—"

Kimo and Ilima spoke at the same instant, breaking off together.

"You first." Kimo nodded at her. The newspaper had fallen off his lap and lay forgotten at his feet, half-hidden under the coffee table.

Ilima hurriedly put the soda can and the plate on the table and brushed off her hands. She stood nervously for a second before taking a deep breath.

"I don't know what you're talking about, Jack. Kimo and I haven't 'found each other.'"

She looked to Kimo for confirmation. He nodded.

"It's your imagination, Jack." Kimo found himself going alternately hot and cold at the thought of becoming involved with his friend's sister. The expectations. The commitment. You couldn't have a casual romance with your best friend's sister. And casual relationships were the only kind Kimo had ever had. He didn't know if he could cope with any other kind.

"We're just friends," Ilima added.

"That's right. Friends." Kimo smiled encouragement at her. "We've been helping each other out. Right, friend?"

"Right."

Ilima suddenly remembered something she had to do. Immediately. "I've got to, uh . . . clean up." She gestured toward the other room. "In the kitchen."

"I'll help."

Kimo hurried after her. They had to talk about this.

As Ilima raced out of the room, Kimo right behind her, Jack's laughter followed.

As soon as they reached the kitchen, Ilima rounded on Kimo, hands fisted on her hips.

"What did you say to Jack?" she demanded.

"Nothing. He was just talking. He looked up at me and just said that . . . what you heard." Kimo didn't even want to repeat it. "I mean, I think we're getting along really well. Working together and all. Helping Jack."

"Right. But that's it, right? You'll be going back to Maui soon."

As Ilima said it, the idea of Kimo's leave-taking brought a stab of pain to her heart. Even though they weren't a couple the way Jack seemed to be thinking, she enjoyed Kimo's company and she was going to miss him.

"That's right." But the thought of returning to Maui brought no joy.

Suddenly Kimo laughed. "Do you notice we seem to be saying 'right' a lot?"

Ilima joined in his laughter. "Right."

The two of them roared. Standing in the kitchen, leaning over and laughing until they dropped tiredly into chairs, they released the tension between them with gales of laughter. Finally, holding her aching stomach muscles, Ilima pulled herself upright and put some effort into sobering up.

"We're just friends, and Jack will just have to take our word for it."

Ilima managed to calm herself, and resisted looking at Kimo in case that started her laughing all over again.

"Why don't you go in and sit with him while I make some sandwiches and some popcorn? Then we can start the movie."

"Good idea." Jack's voice floated in from the door where he stood, leaning casually on his crutches. "I thought you two got lost in here. I'm starved."

While Ilima scolded, asking what had happened to the pastries she'd just given him, the two men left, commiserating over their ideas of women.

Ilima shut the door behind them, leaning for a

moment against the cool wood. They could try to convince Jack that there was nothing between them. They might even succeed. But how on earth was she supposed to convince herself?

Chapter Eight

"Jack." Kimo came in from outdoors on Monday morning, catching his friend leafing desultorily through the morning paper. "I've got an idea. See what you think."

Jack folded the paper over and threw it onto the coffee table. "Anything. Man, I am so bored being cooped up in here."

"That's what I told Ilima. Said I'd take you with me over to the store to pick up a few things."

"Great. Let's go." Jack was already reaching for his crutches when Kimo stopped him.

"Wait. That's not really what I wanted to do." Kimo sat in his usual chair beside the couch, leaning in toward Jack. He kept his voice low. It was unlikely that Ilima would be anywhere near the house, but there was no way to be sure. "Well, we will stop at the store so that she doesn't get suspicious."

Now Jack was watching him with great interest. A spark of life, sadly missing from his eyes lately, was gleaming, making his light brown eyes look astonishingly like Ilima's.

"What I thought we could do is drive around the area—take the path you usually take on your midnight walks."

Jack was getting excited enough to squirm on the sofa. "And I can watch for that van," Jack finished for him. "That's a great idea. Wish I'd thought of it."

It was obvious he wanted to start already, as his hands reached for the crutches, holding them at the ready. But then his eyes clouded and his face turned troubled. "Will Ilima be okay? Being here alone, I mean?"

Kimo nodded. He would never make the suggestion if it meant leaving Ilima in any danger. "Ilima is working in the heliconias again, finishing up the work she started on Saturday. It'll probably take all morning and part of the afternoon. And she has the Mederios brothers out there with her."

Jack's face brightened. "That's right. They're on spring break and wanted to make some extra money. They'll be helping out in the garden all week.'' The two teenagers lived next door, and their mother was a good friend of Ilima's. They worked for the Lyman twins during the summer, and often helped out when they had time off from school. ''They're pretty good workers,'' Jack added, ''and Ilima will be okay with them here. Keanu plays on his school's football team, and he's almost as big as you.''

Kimo grinned. ''I noticed. And his brother looks like he's going to catch up to him pretty soon.''

''No wonder you came up with this plan.'' Jack pushed the crutches into place and stood. ''Let's get going.''

It didn't take them long to settle in the car, though it required some maneuvering on Jack's part. Compact cars and leg casts were not an easy combination.

''So,'' Kimo said, stopping the car at the end of the driveway. ''Where do you usually walk?''

Jack pointed to the right. ''I go up here, and around the corner. Then I just follow the streets in there until I get tired.''

The Lyman land was on a corner, where the highway that ran along the front of their property met a narrow road that led off *mauka*. This was where Jack always began his walks, moving away from the well-traveled highway that could be busy even at one in the morning. Then he followed the twisting roads that led gently upward toward the mountain, moving through the area among the houses and small farms. He enjoyed the solitary time, the quiet of the night hours.

"It looks different in the daylight," he commented now to Kimo. "I don't walk in the daytime; that's when I'm working. But you should see it at night." Jack's voice hummed with enthusiasm as he described his late walks. "The stars are so bright you feel like you can reach out and touch them. And on winter nights when there's snow on the mountains . . . the air is so crisp it almost hurts to breathe. But it's so clean and fresh. . . ."

His voice trailed off as he realized he was starting to ramble. He gave an awkward laugh. "I like the outdoors. I guess you can tell. I hate being cooped up inside all the time." The frustration of the last few days was evident in his voice. "That's why I grow things for a living; so I can be outdoors."

"Hey, you don't have to tell me. I grow things too, remember, even though I spend a lot of time on sales these days. I like the outdoors. I'd be out there with Ilima and her two overgrown boys if I didn't think it was important to get you out of the house for a little while."

"And I appreciate it, man." Jack was beginning to feel embarrassed. First he was getting poetic about nature, and now he was becoming emotional. Must be the head injury.

Kimo, perhaps recognizing how Jack felt, brought back the man-to-man atmosphere with a scolding retort. ''Well, open your window all the way, brudda, and breathe deep. This is all the outdoors you gonna get for now. And keep your eyes open.''

Kimo steered the car up and down the streets, keeping to a strict twenty-five miles per hour so that they could examine any cars parked in driveways and carports.

After some ten minutes of this, Kimo slapped the steering wheel in frustration. ''This isn't going to work. Everyone's at work now.'' He shook his head, wondering how he could have been so dumb.

There were almost no cars to be seen, the exception being a row of rusted-out cars parked to the side of the house they were passing. They were obviously not in working order, since weeds grew up around the tireless wheels almost as high as the car doors. But the majority of the carports and driveways were disappointingly empty.

''Yeah, you might be right,'' Jack reluctantly agreed. ''We should have done this yesterday.''

Kimo sighed. ''I wish I'd thought of it in the morning while Ilima was out. We couldn't have gotten away in the afternoon; and what would we

have done with Ilima if we could have? We can't
leave her alone, that's for sure.''

They had no sooner sat in front of the television
Sunday afternoon than the doorbell had rung. The
visitor turned out to be the first of many. Guard
friends of Jack's, some of the independent flower
growers, even a few of Ilima's girlfriends had all
stopped by to see how Jack was doing. They never
had watched the movie Ilima rented, instead spending the rest of the day with their friends. And by
the time everyone left, Jack was too worn out to
sit through a movie.

''I've been thinking, though.'' Jack's voice was
somber, thoughtful, in accord with his words. ''I
know I've seen that beige van. In fact, I think I've
seen it a lot. When I'm out here walking, it's usually very late. And I'm not talking ten o'clock at
night. When I come out it's usually after midnight.
More often two or three o'clock. There might be a
few cars on the highway, but there aren't many in
here, in the residential area. That's why I remember
that van.''

Kimo frowned, trying to think about what his
friend was saying. ''Maybe he works the night shift
somewhere.''

''Could be. But I'm thinking that I saw him a
lot. Both coming and going.''

''That's strange.''

''Yeah. It doesn't make sense. If he was going to work, or coming home from work, I should have just seen him traveling in one direction all the time.'' He shook his head. ''But then nothing about this whole thing makes sense.''

Jack was still looking out the window, examining the houses they passed, when he turned quickly, almost shouting to Kimo beside him. ''Stop! I think I saw it.''

Kimo stepped on the brake immediately, checked his rearview mirror, and, seeing that there were no cars behind him, backed up. Sure enough, there beside a smallish house with a yard that badly needed mowing was a Dodge van. Beige.

Kimo stopped the car. ''Do you have something to write on?'' he asked Jack, his voice fast and urgent. He read off the license number, squinting to make it out without getting any closer. ''And make a note of the house number. Do you know the name of this street?''

Jack found a pencil and paper in the glove compartment and jotted down the numbers. Kimo had already put the car back into drive and was moving forward. As they reached the end of the street and made their turn, Jack took down the street name.

Then, feeling full of success and male pride, they headed toward the shopping center.

* * *

Ilima lunched at the Mederios' house that day. Her friend Sara prepared a large luncheon for her "growing boys" and invited Ilima to join them. So the men didn't tell her about their short journey into private investigation until that night at dinner.

Ilima was not pleased. She stared at them as though they were exhibits in a zoo, and her voice was almost shrill when she spoke.

"Are you two nuts? Why didn't you call Mel with this idea, or tell the police officers who came over yesterday to check for tire prints?"

Kimo was glad they'd waited until the end of the meal to tell her. He'd put a pot roast in the oven after lunch, then spent the afternoon showing Jack how to use his computer more efficiently. Jack admitted that they just used it for billing, but Kimo insisted their program was capable of much more, and he meant to show him while Jack was housebound. So the meal cooked itself while they worked in the small office down the hall.

Ilima had been enjoying the meal, but she pushed away her plate when she started to rail at them.

"It wasn't dangerous," Jack insisted, and Ilima knew he was exhibiting the stubborn streak he'd gotten from Grandma. "We just drove around a bit."

"It's strange about that van," Kimo told her.

''Jack says he saw it all the time, coming and going, and at some very strange hours. The guy might be working the night shift, but then he wouldn't be going both ways in such a short period of time.''

Ilima frowned. She seemed to be angrier than ever. Kimo wouldn't have been surprised if she'd picked up her plate and flung it across the room; she looked upset enough to do it. When she spoke her voice was tight from the emotion she was holding in check. Not just anger, Kimo realized as she went on. Fear.

''You two have no sense. Keanu and Keoki were talking while we worked. They said all the kids in this area know not to go hiking in the undeveloped land *mauka* of here. Apparently someone has started a small *pakalolo* patch in there, and the boys think it might be dangerous to get too near it.''

All around the islands, not-so-law-abiding types cultivated patches of marijuana in out-of-the-way spots: in the rain forests, in old cane fields, anywhere the natural foliage could help hide and camouflage the illegal plants. Vacant land, overgrown with head-high weeds would serve as well. And it could be dangerous to get too near these hidden gardens; many of them were booby-trapped.

Kimo and Jack both stared at her.

Kimo was the first to recover. ''And you think

that van has something to do with someone growing *pakalolo?*''

''Doesn't it make sense to you that someone doing something illegal might be doing it during hours when most people are sleeping?'' She looked pointedly at Jack. She'd wanted him to get medical help for his sleep problems, but he'd insisted on struggling through on his own.

Jack looked guilty. ''I'm sorry, Ilima, Kimo. This whole thing is my fault. If I didn't go out wandering around in the middle of the night, none of this would have happened.'' He crumpled his paper napkin and dropped it on the table beside his plate.

''And the whole thing is so stupid.'' Frustration showed in every line of his lean body. ''Because if what you're saying is true, then whoever drives that van must have thought I knew all this. And wanted to get rid of me because of it.''

Ilima shuddered at the calm manner Jack was speaking about something that sounded a lot like cold-blooded murder.

''And the thing is,'' Jack continued, ''I don't know a thing. I don't know who drives the van, don't even care. I doubt if I ever saw the driver. I don't really pay attention to stuff like that when I'm walking.''

He frowned. He used his walking time to fight his inner demons, a fact he wasn't exactly eager to share. Kimo—and maybe even Ilima—understood this, but he still felt embarrassed to say it out loud.

"I try to clear my mind and appreciate nature. I like to see the stars and smell the cool night air. Sometimes there's a light drizzle and I like that too. It makes everything smell so fresh and clean."

He shook his head to clear it, aware that he was getting into personal areas he'd as soon keep private. "My mind is so far off when I'm walking that I'm surprised I even remember seeing that darn van at all."

Ilima stood up, rushing to her brother's side to give him a hug. He reached up, capturing her hand on his shoulder with his and giving it a squeeze. Ilima couldn't help but remember the last time she'd tried to offer her help, here in this same room, and been so rudely rebuffed. Her lips parted in a grin at this further indication of Jack's recovery.

"You know the funny part?" Jack looked at both Ilima and Kimo, a sardonic grin on his lips. "The accident seems to have knocked those nightmares right out of my head. I haven't had a single one since the accident. I've been sleeping well too, even though I told the doctor I didn't want any sleep aids."

Ilima gave him another hug, her pale eyes glittering with a sudden dampness. "That's wonderful, Jack. Maybe it means that you'll be fine now. I'm sure it does," she amended.

"It proves what they say about silver linings," Kimo remarked. He pushed his plate away and folded his arms, leaning forward to rest them on the table. "I guess we should call Mel and run all this by him. See what he says."

"Great idea," Ilima said. "I feel so much better."

Deciding there was no urgency now that she knew the call would be made, she returned to her place at the table. Resuming her seat, she looked brightly at the two men. "Is there any dessert?"

Jack laughed. "Working hard must have made her hungry."

Kimo smiled. "You're in luck. Jack made *haupia.*"

Ilima's brows shot up. "*Jack* did?"

Her eyes moved from Kimo to Jack. Her brother shrugged. Ilima noted the small gesture with a catch in her heart. Kimo did that all the time. Jack must have picked it up from his friend.

"Kimo taught me. It was easy." Shifting in his chair at the continued incredulous look he was getting from his sister, Jack shrugged again. "I had to do something a little more active after slaving over the computer all afternoon. Even if it was just moving around the kitchen with Kimo.''

Due to his awkwardness because of the crutches, Jack allowed Kimo to serve the gelatinlike coconut pudding. Ilima raved over it, embarrassing Jack a little. But she could see how proud he was of his achievement as well. She was proud of him too. Kimo was affecting their lives in many different ways. And while she wasn't sure all of them were good, many were. If she spent the rest of the week in the gardens with the Mederios brothers, maybe she could manage to stay far enough away from Kimo to appreciate his good qualities more.

Though actually, she realized, her problem was that she appreciated Kimo *too* much. There had to be some way for her to recapture her earlier attitude toward him as valued family friend. She'd just have to scold herself whenever she found that she was looking at him in a romantic light.

Ilima smiled grimly at the two men enjoying their dessert and laughing together over something Jack had done on the computer that afternoon. Remembering their foolish pride over their investigative trip this morning was enough to make her shiver with fear.

She came to a decision. Whenever she felt even

slightly romantic over Kimo, she'd have to remember how infuriating and irresponsible and childish men could be. Her lips turned up in a decisive grin. That should do it.

Chapter Nine

Jack and Kimo talked to Mel later that evening. To Ilima's delight, he too scolded them for taking things into their own hands.

"Investigating on your own that way could have been very dangerous. These people have already tried to kill Jack," he reminded them. "You should have called me with your proposal. We could have sent someone out to drive over your regular walking route with you."

Ilima tried hard not to say "I told you so," but she did allow herself a private smile at the remorseful looks Jack and Kimo wore when they got off the phone.

* * *

The next morning, Mel came out to the house and talked to Jack and Kimo again. Then he found Ilima, Keanu, and Keoki in the gardens and spoke to them. He spent a lot of time asking the two boys about anything they'd heard concerning illegal activities in the vicinity. At first they were reticent, reluctant to "tell tales." But with patient questioning, they were able to provide him with names of friends who lived *mauka* and might have further information.

Feeling subdued by everyone's fear about their mission the previous day, Jack and Kimo spent the day indoors. After a rocky start on Monday, Jack had taken to the computer, absorbing all the information Kimo had to impart and anxious for more. Once he'd gone over the business applications, Kimo showed Jack how to connect to the Internet, and went on to instruct him on how to create a web site for Lyman Flowers.

The rest of the week passed slowly while they waited for the wheels of justice to turn. Ilima, Jack, and Kimo found out later that the police were very busy while the three of them spent a tense week trying to keep occupied with work and wondering what was going to happen. They tried to continue a normal business routine, but thoughts of the beige van and a scruffy peeping Tom were never far away.

On Wednesday morning, Ilima and Kimo found themselves alone together in the truck on their way to Hilo for the farmers' market. Ilima shook her head as they made the turn at Keaau.

"Tell me again how Jack talked us into this."

Kimo, handling the driving, grinned. "He was pretty slick, I'll give him that." He shook his head in appreciation. "He must have been up all night figuring out how to con us into going in and leaving him at home."

"He'll be okay though, won't he?" Now that they were a few miles down the road, Ilima couldn't understand how she'd agreed to leave Jack.

"Of course he'll be all right. I had a few words with Keanu and Keoki before we left. They'll look out for him."

Feeling a little better, Ilima let her mind go back to the early morning hours, when she had joined Kimo in the carport to cut the flowers for the morning's farmers' market. Jack was there before either of them. He stood on his good leg, balancing the crutches under his arms. He also had a lawn chair rigged with a piece of nylon rope so that he could sling it over his back and carry it about.

"What . . . ?" Ilima gazed at him, speechless.

Kimo looked over the rope and chair with interest. "Hey, brudda. What's with the rig-up?"

Jack smiled proudly at them both. "I can't take any more of this being cooped up indoors all the time," he told them. "So I'm going to show you that I can manage okay outside. Go on," he urged, "you two just go on and cut the flowers. I'm going to show you what I came up with."

"Jack . . ." Ilima began, but was forestalled by Kimo, who laid a hand on her back and urged her forward. He took the clippers they'd need in one hand, passing a pair of gloves to Ilima with his other.

"Come on, Ilima. Shall we start with the ginger?"

So they'd moved out into the early morning light, walking toward the first of the plant beds. Birds in the garden were beginning to sing, and from several houses away they could just hear a rooster crow. Next door a dog barked.

Jack followed Kimo and Ilima, enjoying the fresh, cool air, glad to be outside.

When Kimo and Ilima stopped beside the tall red ginger stalks, ready to cut the first flowers, Jack took the chair from his back, set it up with a quick flick of his wrist, and sat down. A triumphant smile lit his features as Ilima and Kimo watched with tentative grins.

"See?" Jack almost crowed in delight. "I can move around the gardens and direct Keanu and Keoki. I can sit and watch what they're doing; and talk a little with someone other than you two. Not that you two aren't fun to talk to," he hastened to add. "And best of all, I get to be outside for a while."

Kimo could see the frown gathering across Ilima's forehead, could almost see the fear in her eyes. Would Jack be too vulnerable outdoors? He rushed to speak before she could raise an objection.

"It's not a bad idea. Fresh air and a little sun will probably be good for you," he told Jack. He turned to Ilima. "Don't you think so?"

Ilima didn't. She wanted Jack safely inside, away from danger. But she also knew that the ten days he'd already spent indoors were too much for him. "Well, I guess some fresh air would be good," she conceded.

Jack's smile was reward enough, she decided. "But only this morning," she added.

Jack had no problem with that. "That's just what I thought. Just this morning so that you two could go to the market together. It will be good for you to get out too, Ilima. You've been cooped up with me too, after all."

"Oh, no," Ilima was quick to object. "I've been working outside almost every day."

But Jack was shaking his head. "I know that. But that's all you've been doing—working. Working in the gardens, looking after me. You need to get out a bit. So I thought if I could handle the supervisory chores here this morning, you and Kimo could go to the farmers' market and then stop somewhere for lunch. Make a morning of it. Then I'll be a good boy and take a nap when you get back."

His grin was so irrepressible they had to grin back. And now they were in the loaded truck and halfway to Hilo.

They arrived in plenty of time to get set up before any of Ilima's regular customers arrived. Not that there was a lot of setting up to do. The farmers' market in Hilo was a twice-weekly event held under white tents on an intersection in the historic downtown area. The tents remained up throughout the week, and all they had to do was set out the buckets of flowers, a couple of chairs, and the small table where Ilima kept the cash box.

They had an ideal spot along the sidewalk that edged Kamehameha Avenue. Beside Ilima were several other growers selling plants and flowers; behind them were long tables filled with all manner of fruits and vegetables. Across Mamo Street there were more tents, these filled with vendors offering things as diverse as bamboo furniture, T-shirts, and jewelry. And, always, more flowers.

It was a beautiful morning, the sun shining, the mountains clear and blue. Kimo and Ilima kept busy with the tourists and sightseers. All her regulars came for their bouquets, taking time to inquire about Jack and offer their good wishes.

Between customers, Kimo and Ilima sat and talked and laughed together. On the other side of busy Kamehameha Avenue they could see Mo'oheau Park and the old bandstand. Beyond that, the Pacific was as calm as its name implied.

Ilima had never felt so comfortable with a man. Except for Jack, of course, and he didn't count. She and Kimo seemed to have endless things to say to each other; yet they were also able to sit together for long moments of silence without feeling the obligation to talk.

At noon, they gathered up their few remaining bouquets and repacked the truck.

''Should we really stay long enough to have lunch?''

Ilima had enjoyed the morning, but her anxiety over Jack was flooding back.

Kimo wanted to spend the extra time with her, but he understood her concern. He compromised. ''Maybe we could pick up *bento* lunches somewhere.''

Ilima responded with a brilliant smile. "What a great idea! I know a wonderful sushi place. And it's right on the way home."

So they picked up their box lunches in Hilo, but ended up stopping at a park on the way back to eat. Ilima had wanted to drive straight through and eat at home, but Kimo convinced her Jack would feel insulted if they rushed back without eating.

"I'm glad you made me stop," Ilima told him, as they sat under a flowering shower tree and ate their lunches. From time to time the delicate petals drifted down around them like sporadic yellow raindrops. "It's beautiful here, and I'm even managing to relax."

"Then I'm glad too." Kimo finished up his food and reached for the Spam *musubi* left on Ilima's plate. "I'm sorry it took Jack's accident to get me here but I'm real glad I came, Ilima. I'm glad I got to know you better."

Ilima was laughing.

Kimo, truly baffled, tried not to look hurt. He was trying to be sincere and she was laughing at him? He finished chewing his mouthful of rice and Spam and swallowed. "What?"

"I said 'I'm glad,' and then you repeated it three or four times. All in the same sentence."

Kimo's expression changed from hurt to humor.

"Did I? I guess that tells you how I feel, though." He was grinning widely.

"No," Ilima teased. "How do you feel?"

Kimo rolled over, grabbing her around the waist. She ended up flat on her back in the grass, Kimo sprawled alongside her. But his fingers remained at her waist, tickling her.

"No, no." She swatted ineffectually at his hands, laughing uncontrollably. "Okay, I give up."

Laughing himself, Kimo leaned over her, stilling his hands, smiling into her eyes. "So how do I feel?"

"You feel *glad*!" she exclaimed, the words almost lost in her merry laughter.

Kimo's eyes remained on hers, but his expression grew serious. "You're so beautiful, you know."

His wonderful words sobered her too. "No, I'm not."

He smiled. "I'm not going to let you turn this into a childish argument."

He reached out and brushed a curl back, away from her eyes. His fingers were light on her skin, sending shivers down her spine.

"I, uh, think we should be heading home." Ilima nervously ran the tip of her tongue over suddenly dry lips.

Kimo took another moment to look into her face.

His gaze had locked on her lips, and she repressed the urge to moisten them yet again with her tongue.

Ilima held her breath. He was so close. Would he lean in just a little farther? Would he touch her lips with his?

But after a silence almost deep enough for her to hear her own heartbeat, Kimo pushed himself up.

"I guess we should."

Once he had risen, Kimo held out a hand to help her up. Ilima looked into his eyes for an instant, then placed her hand in his. Warmth shot through her, not just into the hand he held but throughout her body as her blood raced through her veins. She stood, pulling her hand away from his quickly to dust off her clothes. She was sure he'd wanted to kiss her; yet he hadn't. Self-consciously she bent to gather up their trash.

Kimo was quick to help with the cleanup. He deposited the various bits and pieces in the barrel marked RUBBISH. Then he took her hand and held on to it until they reached the truck. He helped her get into the cab. "It was a nice morning, Ilima. One of the best I can remember."

As Ilima hesitated, searching for the proper words to reply to such a lovely compliment, Kimo shut the door and headed around the car to the driver's seat. By the time he'd fastened his seat belt and started the engine, he appeared to be a million miles away. The opportunity for a reply was lost. So Ilima wrapped herself in memories of their pleasant morning. And they drove back in silence.

Chapter Ten

Finally, it was over. Mel called them just before the news came on that Thursday evening.

"Jack. We have the van that hit you. No doubt about it." Mel sounded tired, but there was no mistaking the pleasure in his voice. He was happy to be able to relay this news to Jack. "That van you and Kimo saw on your drive on Monday was the one that hit you. We also have reason to believe the man who owns it is responsible for a *pakalolo* field out in the hills not too far from his place. There may be a report on the evening news—about our destroying the field. So I wanted to let you know first. I'll drop in tomorrow to tell you all about it."

After the call from Mel, they made sure to watch

the news together that evening. The report Mel mentioned was broadcast, detailing the discovery and destruction of a *pakalolo* field in the Puna area. Arrests had been made. Other charges were pending.

Mel arrived at midmorning on Friday. Ilima had gotten Keanu and Keoki started on their morning's work, then came in to make a pot of coffee in anticipation of his visit. Jack proudly produced his latest culinary effort, a loaf of Portuguese sweet bread. They sat in the living room enjoying the bread and coffee as they talked. Or rather, Mel talked. The others mostly listened.

"Despite the danger involved, your detective work really paid off," he told Jack and Kimo. As the two men exchanged smug smiles, Mel fixed them with a stern look. "You still should *not* have done it, but once we had a vehicle to check out, it was easy to determine it was the car involved in your hit-and-run."

"Did you find out why they did it?"

Jack and Kimo both shushed Ilima.

"Let the man tell it his own way," Jack told her.

Mel smiled. "It's pretty much what Jack worked out after he heard your suspicions about *pakalolo*. There were four people involved—two men, cousins, and their girlfriends. Though the women were just charged as accessories. They had nothing to do with your accident.''

Mel paused long enough to take a long drink of coffee before resuming his narrative. ''The guys would work on their crop during the day, but a lot of the activity was done at night. One of them worked the night shift at the hospital. So some of the coming and going was legitimate. But once they harvested their crop they moved the stuff around at night. That's when you saw all the comings and goings,'' he told Jack.

''I wonder why they did it at night,'' Kimo said. ''It seems to me it would look even more suspicious—all that moving around so late at night.''

Jack nodded his agreement.

Mel agreed. ''I think so too. But remember, most of these guys aren't real smart. Sometimes they do silly things because it seems like something they should be doing. You know, like having a password or a secret meeting place. It makes them feel more like big shots, I suppose.'' He shrugged. ''It's okay with me. That's the kind of mistake that lets us catch them.''

''So they thought I was watching them?'' Jack asked.

''They kept seeing you on the streets, night after night. I guess neither of them has any trouble sleeping.'' He grinned at Jack. ''Anyway, they couldn't figure out why you were out there night after night. They finally decided you must be spying on them. Though from what they've said, the hit-and-run itself was a purely impetuous act. They saw you there on the corner ahead of them that morning. There was no other traffic, no one around. It was a simple thing just to veer off to the shoulder and hit you. Then they continued on their way. They didn't know how badly you were hurt. Didn't care at that point.''

Ilima had gone white at the matter-of-fact tone Mel used to recite the facts of the case.

Jack was a little pale himself. ''What about the incident at the hospital? If one of them worked there . . . ?''

''That's right,'' Kimo agreed. ''That's what really got you looking into the accident, after all.''

Mel nodded. ''It did seem like too much of a coincidence—this guy working at the hospital. He's a maintenance man, does cleaning and odd jobs. Changes lightbulbs, stuff like that. Or rather, he did.'' Mel grinned. ''I think it will be a while before he's out of jail.''

Jack and Kimo cheered, but Ilima just listened. The sweet bread lay half-eaten on her plate; the plate sat forgotten on the end table beside her chair. Her mug was still gripped tightly in her hands, but Kimo doubted she knew it was there.

"But was it?" she asked. "Coincidence?"

Mel nodded again, taking a sip of his coffee. "Amazing, isn't it? But apparently it was. No one tried to kill you in the hospital, Jack. The doctor called us in because of the hit-and-run, of course. When there appeared to be a problem over your medication, he thought there might be a connection. But I've been working with the hospital on this; they did their own investigation. It seems there was a young nurse on duty that night, not long out of school, working a double shift. And having emotional problems at home too. Kind of a triple whammy. It was an honest mistake on her part. She switched two of the syringes and gave you the wrong medication. We're all just lucky it wasn't a fatal mistake for you or the other patient."

Ilima let out her breath. So that hadn't been a murder attempt after all. It was a relief to hear it. Belatedly, she realized she still held the mug of cooling coffee, and put it down on an end table.

But her relief was short-lived as she remembered that those men *had* tried to kill Jack. Impulsive or not, they had hit him and caused him serious harm. They didn't know he was still alive; they'd just driven off, left him for dead.

Mel had more to tell, recounting how they'd watched the van for a few days before impounding it in the accident investigation. That was how they'd uncovered the *pakalolo* field. "Though the police out here had heard about it and were working on it. If it wasn't for the accident, they might have taken longer, though. We managed to push things forward because of the additional charges."

"Why was that guy peering in the window that day?" Kimo asked. More than anything, that incident had bothered him. Even with his leg in a cast, Kimo felt Jack could take care of himself. But the peeping Tom incident had endangered Ilima.

Mel explained. "Joe—he's the one who worked at the hospital—saw you there just before you checked out," he told Jack. "He got panicky and talked his cousin into bringing him over here. He *says* he was just looking around, trying to be sure you were all right."

Kimo laughed. "Yeah. Right."

Jack looked bemused.

Ilima just listened. She was having trouble believing it was all finally over.

Mel checked his watch. "I want to go out and thank your young helpers," he told Ilima. "The information they provided was a big help."

Ilima checked her own watch and directed Mel next door. "It's just about lunchtime. They'll be heading home. Sara always has a big meal ready for them."

All three of them walked Mel to the door, thanking him again for all he had done. After he left, Ilima encompassed Jack in a big bear hug. He might be bigger than she was, but she still felt able to mother him a little. They'd always been close, the result of growing up with young, self-centered parents. And then there had only been their elderly grandparents, and not even a grandfather for too long. They'd had to rely on themselves, and Ilima had naturally fallen into the nurturing role, while Jack had taken upon himself their protection—from what, Ilima had never asked.

"I'm so glad it's over," she told him now.

Jack returned her hug, not even a little self-conscious over the emotional exchange. Kimo came up and added a hug of his own, managing to enclose both of them in his embrace.

Ilima felt a little shiver up her spine as Kimo's arm wrapped around her. She ignored it. This was a special moment. They were all safe. She wouldn't let her feelings and doubts about Kimo get mixed up in it.

Later that afternoon Jack and Ilima were together in the office going over some records on the computer when Kimo came in, his eyes troubled. He'd called his parents on Maui, catching them up on what was happening on the big island.

''I can't believe it,'' he told Jack and Ilima now. ''But Geoff is still at my place.''

Ilima looked up. ''Your friend who was visiting from England?''

Kimo nodded.

''I thought he was going back last week?''

''So did I.'' Kimo rubbed his hand across his face. He looked tired and not a little guilty. ''He was supposed to leave on Wednesday—two days after I arrived here. I got my niece Lilia to kind of watch out for him for those two days. But then he came down with the chicken pox.''

''Chicken pox?'' Jack looked up from the screen, a grin on his face. ''Geoff has the chicken pox? How old is he anyway?'' he asked, laughing. ''I thought he was our age.''

Ilima eyed Jack. ''Adults can get the chicken pox. They usually get it worse than kids do.''

Kimo nodded. ''That's what happened. My folks were having their fiftieth wedding anniversary party right after he arrived, and I took him over to meet everyone. We had a good time. Geoff even played some games with the kids.''

''Uh-oh.'' Ilima couldn't hide a grin.

''Uh-oh for sure. The day after the party one of the little cousins came down with it. Lilia's daughter got it right after I left, and I guess Geoff got it the next day.'' He rubbed his face over again, his hand passing over his mouth and chin before resting for a moment on his neck. "He must have been getting it already when I left. I remember him saying he thought he was coming down with a cold, and how hard it would be flying with a head cold. He was supposed to go on to Australia and New Zealand from here, then head back to England."

Ilima did some mental arithmetic. "But it's been twelve days now. Surely he must be recovered."

"Well, you were right about adults getting it worse. Apparently Mealoha is all well and back to her old self. But Geoff was sick in bed for several days, and he's just now feeling better."

"Wow." Jack had gotten over his initial humor and was showing his concern. "So he's okay now?"

Kimo nodded.

"I guess you'll have to be getting back." Ilima felt her heart twist. She'd known Kimo would be returning to Maui, and probably soon. But the reality of it was a surprisingly physical blow.

"Yes." Kimo didn't sound too anxious. "I'll call the airlines and see if I can get on this afternoon's flight."

"About time," Jack said, a smile on his lips but not in his eyes. He was just as sad to see Kimo leave, Ilima knew. "I've been wanting to kick you out of my room," he said.

Kimo, on his way out of the room to use the kitchen phone, stopped long enough to slap Jack on the back. "I'm gonna miss you too, bro." He stopped a minute, staring down at the cast still covering most of Jack's leg. "I think you should stay over here in the house until that cast comes off, though."

Ilima hurried to second this. "Kimo's right, Jack. It's still awkward for you, getting around. Even though you're doing so much more. And you should be getting a smaller cast in a week or two."

Jack reluctantly agreed—he knew he wouldn't be able to manage in the tiny bathroom off his own room.

"Be sure to tell Geoff hello from me. And that I'm glad he's recovered."

Kimo moved into the kitchen to call the airlines, and Ilima turned to the window. She stood staring out at the cars moving along the highway. They had a lot of frontage, planted with some of their loveliest tropical flowers. She was used to the hum of the traffic, almost welcomed the familiar noise of it. But for once the steady hum of tires, the chatter of the birds, and the peace of the garden did nothing to soothe her spirit. Her heart was breaking, and she knew why. Knew, but hated to admit it. Actually saying it, even just to herself, was so . . . definite.

She was in love with Kimo.

Ilima didn't know when it had happened, but she thought it might have been as early as that first day. Perhaps when he took her into his arms at the hospital and lent the comfort of his warm embrace. Or it might have been when he took her to the church to light a candle for Jack's recovery. Then again, it might have been later . . . perhaps when he surprised her with the pancake breakfast that first morning. Or when he offered to take the flowers to the farmers' market that first Wednesday.

What she realized, thinking back, was that he had done so many things for her since the moment of his arrival that it was impossible to pick out any one as the definitive action that had made her love him. He was always so considerate, always trying to make things easier for her—and for Jack. He'd done so much for both of them. Special things. Wonderful things.

But while she might love him, Ilima knew he didn't love her. ''Just friends.'' That was what they'd told Jack. She knew it was what Kimo believed.

''Well, I'm all set.'' Kimo strolled back into the room, a grin on his face, but his eyes still troubled. He looked over to Ilima, but she refused to meet his eyes. She turned toward him, but her gaze centered somewhere in the vicinity of his right ear.

"Do you need any help getting your things together?"

Kimo looked at Ilima. She was so beautiful standing there against the window. Her hair was a halo that glowed almost gold from the backlight, but he couldn't see her eyes, those glorious apple-cider eyes. Would they be filled with sadness to see him go?

"Thanks, but I can manage. I didn't bring much. You'll take me to the airport, though, won't you?"

"Sure," Jack and Ilima both answered at the same time.

"Well . . ." Kimo tried again to meet Ilima's gaze, to see what her reaction was to his going. Again, he could not. "I guess I'd better go get my stuff together."

With one last hopeless glance toward Ilima, he walked out of the room.

Jack, still seated at the computer, watched them both, his head moving back and forth like a spectator at a tennis match.

Ilima glared at him. "What are you doing?"

Jack met her eyes, full of brotherly concern. "What are *you* two doing?" He looked after Kimo for a moment, then turned back to his sister. "You two are made for each other. I don't know why you refuse to admit it. I can see it in your eyes when you look at each other. Man, there's love shining through. But you've got Grandma's stubborn streak, and for some reason you refuse to admit that you love him.''

Ilima sat beside her brother. She grasped her hands together before her, dropping them into her lap between her knees. ''We're just friends, Jack.'' Maybe if she said it often enough she'd come to believe it too. ''Kimo doesn't love me. He's handsome and happy and without a care in the world. He could have anyone he wanted, Jack, but he doesn't. Because he doesn't want to settle down. He's happy the way he is.''

Jack's eyes widened. ''Boy, I guess love is blind.'' He shook his head at his sister. ''Can't you see how great a husband he would be? He likes all that domestic stuff.''

It was Ilima's turn to shake her head. ''We spent a lot of time together, Jack. It was nice. We enjoy each other's company. We're friends. But that's all.''

Her voice indicated that the discussion was over. She stood, leaned down to give her brother a kiss on the cheek, then straightened. ''Thanks for your concern, Jack. But it'll be all right.'' And she walked out of the room.

Chapter Eleven

"Kimo! How are you?" Ilima's voice carried the joy she felt at hearing from him.

It was Friday evening, a week after Kimo's departure. It had been a long week for Ilima, as she labored to get used to life without Kimo's help. Always self-sufficient, she'd needed every ounce of determination to move on after his two-week visit. Jack was still unable to do any of his usual work, and the Mederios brothers had returned to school. Until Jack could find them some temporary help, she had twice the workload. The one good thing in all of this was that, most of the time, she was too busy even to think. But she still had time to miss Kimo.

She savored the sound of his voice now as she listened to his reply to her initial question.

"I'm fine. Working hard. Catching up."

He'd been back home on the slopes of Haleakala for seven days, and although he was working hard, the exhaustion he felt came more from his missing the woman on the other end of the phone line than from any physical work he was doing on the protea farm.

"How's your friend?"

"Geoff's doing well. He's almost recovered. Got lots of spots still, though."

He laughed and Ilima could hear the sound of another male voice speaking in the background.

Kimo's voice held his laughter when he came back on the line. "He says he's still handsomer than me, even with spots."

Ilima laughed too.

"I still cook better, though."

Ilima wasn't sure if he was speaking to her or to his guest. She decided to reply anyway.

"I'm sure you do. I'd like to meet your spotty guest sometime."

Kimo said some words she couldn't hear, apparently speaking to Geoff in the room with him. When he returned to Ilima his voice was soft—speculative. "You just might."

While Ilima wondered just what that might mean, Kimo asked to speak to Jack, and she passed the phone to her brother. Jack had been standing at her elbow for most of the conversation, coming in from the other room as soon as he heard her say Kimo's name.

''Hey, brudda . . .''

Ilima stepped quietly into the other room, giving Jack some privacy to talk to Kimo and Geoff. It had been a long seven days since Kimo left. It was amazing how empty the house seemed without him. She and Jack had lived here alone for over five years, since Grandma's death, and they had never been lonely. Until now. It was a small house, but comfortable, and they both loved it. It was the only home either of them had ever known.

Ilima moved into her bedroom. This had been their grandparents' room. She had moved in after Grandma's death, and her tiny childhood bedroom at the front of the house had become their office.

She looked around the room now. There was no longer any trace of Grandma. She'd painted the walls a soothing apple green, and decorated them with prints of tropical flowers done in delicate watercolors. Ivory curtains covered the window, drawn now over the chill rain. The room had always been her comfort, her refuge, when she was worried about Jack and his trips abroad with the

Guard; when she heard him leaving in the wee hours for his long walks. . . . This was where she would come, snuggle down into the old afghan Grandma had made for her, and read novels, or just daydream.

Funny, she hadn't read a novel since the accident. While Jack was unconscious in the hospital, she hadn't been able to concentrate on anything as casual as a novel, preferring the mindlessness of television movies. And then too, Kimo had been there. Why read a novel when she had hero material right there before her?

Ilima sighed. She sat at the head of the bed, pushing the pillows into a mound behind her. Then she pulled up Grandma's afghan. It was getting old now, the yarn pilling and snagged. But she still loved the old crocheted blanket. It had once been bright with rainbow-colored yarns that reminded her of the colorful gardens Grandma toiled in all day. Now the colors had faded, but the piece as a whole was still beautiful, in her eyes.

Jack poked his head in as soon as he got off the phone. "Hey, guess what?"

Ilima pulled herself out of her memories and managed to find a smile for her brother. He was certainly happy. "What?"

"Kimo is going to come for our birthday."

"Yeah?" Ilima's smile was real now. Their

shared birthday was only two weeks away. "Great."

Jack grinned. "He says he'll cook us a nice meal. He thinks he's a better cook than we are."

Ilima laughed. "That's because he is."

Jack had been doing more in the kitchen, another thing Ilima had to thank Kimo for. He'd been preparing some easy meals Kimo was teaching him to fix via their daily e-mail communication. But he couldn't match his friend's ability. Still, she was glad to be relieved of full-time kitchen duty. And his cooking was at least as good as her own.

Jack laughed with her before he headed back to the office and the computer. Jack had discovered that he had a real flair for working on the computer. He'd put all their business records on disk and had started compiling files on the types of plants they grew, and timetables for their care; he was talking about adding things like yield records, keeping track of the numbers of blossoms cut and sold. He'd also spent much of the past week designing their web site, though he told her he would need a lot more time to get it up and running.

Ilima settled back into her comfortable nest. She was glad Jack was so taken with the computer. She didn't mind doing the business records on it, but she had no desire to get any more involved. Let Jack fool with it all he wanted. And it had the added advantage of keeping him occupied well into the night.

Kimo had also introduced him to computer games, and Jack was well and truly hooked. Even though he wasn't having the sleep problems that had caused them all so much pain, he often stayed up late playing with the computer.

Ilima released a deep sigh. Yet another thing Kimo had done for them. She pulled out a book and held it open on her lap, but she wasn't reading. It was window dressing, in case Jack came back. She really just wanted to sit here and dream; to think about Kimo and what might have been. To remember their good times together; to relive a special kiss. Her lips tipped upward in a smile as she thought of the fun they had cutting flowers together at dawn.

Ilima pulled the afghan up a little higher on her shoulder. It would be so much nicer to be sitting wrapped in Kimo's arms. On a cold and dreary night like this one, he would keep her warm. Together they could listen to the rain pounding on the tin roof, and the steady rhythm would lull them to sleep.

Ilima sighed. Forgetting pretense, she closed the book, putting it down beside her on the bed. She missed Kimo. Throughout the days as she weeded and trimmed and fertilized, she fought constant thoughts of the tall man who had come to help a friend and had ended up stealing her heart.

But he was coming back soon. For her birthday. A smile lit her face.

Well, for Jack's birthday. But since they shared that day, they would be able to share Kimo too.

Ilima's smile grew wider and her eyes sparkled. She'd just had a wonderful idea, an idea that would involve working together with Kimo. She gathered the afghan in her arms, clutching the wool to her chest. It was a terrific idea. And she couldn't wait to get started organizing it.

Ilima was unable to begin putting her plan into action until that Sunday afternoon. In what had become a weekly tradition, a group of Jack's Guard buddies had dropped by for a visit with him. Ilima set them up with drinks and snacks, then took the cordless phone and retreated to her bedroom. She closed the door and turned on the radio before dialing Kimo's number.

"Oh, please let him be there," she mumbled as the phone on Maui rang several times. She released her breath with a loud sigh when she heard his voice say hello.

If he was surprised to hear from her, she wasn't able to tell from his voice. But she did fancy she could hear the special warmth in his voice that indicated his pleasure in her unexpected call.

"Ilima. It's great to hear from you."

She tried to keep her voice low, though Jack and his buddies were talking loudly in the other room. The mellow tones of Israel Kamakawiwo'ole issued from the radio on her night stand, also helping to camouflage her words from those in the other room.

"Jack told me you're going to come over for our birthdays at the end of the month," she began.

Kimo might not have actually asked why she was calling, but she knew he was wondering. They'd spent a lot of time together in the two weeks he'd spent with them, and she felt she could hear the unspoken nuances in his voice.

"Did he tell you about the dinner?"

"Yes, he did. And about the slur on my cooking abilities." Ilima tried to sound stern, but she couldn't hide the laughter in her voice.

"Hey, I'm just trying to be nice, coming over to fix you a gourmet meal."

"Wow. Gourmet, huh?"

Ilima thought it was time to introduce her fabulous plan. The laughter left her voice. Time for more serious business.

"I'm calling because I had an idea after Jack told me about the dinner. What do you think of setting up a surprise party for Jack? I could get him out of the house while you're cooking, and his friends could all come in then, before we get back. They would probably all like to see him again, to see how much he's recovered. And I'd like him to keep in touch with his friends.''

Her voice faltered, steadied, and went on. ''I never realized how many friends he has. All those people who came to visit after the accident. And the cards and all. He's always been so private—so alone. I'd like to help him keep up with everyone, if I can.''

''That's a great idea.'' Kimo was enthusiastic. ''Not just the party, but all of it. Wish I'd thought of it myself. I can tell him I want you two out of the house while I create my culinary masterpiece.''

Ilima laughed. She never laughed as much as when Kimo was around. It felt good. She was too young to be serious all the time.

''Well, it's off to a good start.'' She told him about the Guard friends who were in the living room right now, laughing and playing cards. ''Two or three have been coming every Sunday. I hope they keep it going.''

They spoke for a few minutes longer, about plans for the party and who Ilima would invite. When she hung up the phone, Ilima felt a rush of happiness. It would be such fun to plan this party. And in less than two weeks Kimo would be back in Puna.

In Kula, Kimo hung up the phone, then just stood in the kitchen and stared out the window. He didn't see the green slopes of the mountain, or the yellow blossoms on the plumeria tree in his backyard. Instead he saw a strong face with intriguing uptilted brown eyes the color of apple cider, the whole framed by flyaway wisps of red-gold hair.

In two weeks he'd see Ilima again. He'd thought long and hard before offering to visit for the twins' birthday. But in the end he knew he'd take any excuse to visit them again. To see Ilima again.

He liked her idea about the party for Jack. In fact, he had a few ideas on that score himself. But what had him brooding out the window was the information she'd provided about Jack's friends who were hanging around every Sunday. He had to wonder . . . were they really there to visit Jack? Or did they come so they could see Ilima?

Kimo turned on the faucet and filled a glass with cold water. But he stood there holding it instead of drinking. He had a thirst, all right. But he didn't think the water was going to do much to quench it. In two short weeks Ilima Lyman had become essential to his life. And he had to decide what he was going to do about it.

*   *   *

On Monday afternoon Kimo called Jack. If it wasn't raining on the big island, Ilima was sure to be outside working in the gardens.

"Hey, brudda," Kimo said. "I had an idea over the weekend, after we talked. Are you there alone?"

"Ilima's outside. She's putting in some new ti plants Sara brought over for her. You know, Keoki and Keanu's mom. You should see them. The plants, I mean. Deep reds, some streaked. Great stuff."

Although Jack spoke for a few minutes, and with enthusiasm, about the new plants, he couldn't hide the question in his voice. What could his friend have to say that he couldn't say around Ilima? Or did he want to talk *about* her? A slow smile spread over Jack's face. Had his old friend finally realized that Ilima was pretty special?

"So, did you want to talk about Ilima, then?"

"Yeah, I did. I was thinking it would be kind of nice to surprise Ilima with a party—for her birthday. Get her girlfriends to come over and surprise her, you know? Kind of a thank-you for everything she did for you when you were sick."

"That's a great idea, man." Jack's smile had grown wider. It was surely a good indication of his friend's feelings that this idea had come from him and not from Jack. "Wish I'd thought of it myself."

Kimo was having trouble keeping his laughter contained as he heard what was almost an exact replay of his conversation with Ilima the day before.

"Ilima doesn't get out enough," Jack was saying. "This will be a nice way for her to get together with her friends. I know a couple of her old school friends. I'll get on the phone with them and set it all up. They can tell me who else to invite."

"Good. And when I get there that day, I'll tell her I want the house to myself to work on dinner. So you take her out somewhere—the movies or something. Then her friends can come in while I'm there and hide out. What do you think?"

"Sounds great, man. I can't wait to see her face."

"Me too."

But Kimo was smiling widely when he hung up the phone a few minutes later. He couldn't wait to see Jack's face either.

Chapter Twelve

Ilima grew nervous as she drove down the highway, approaching their house. Kimo had arrived on the early morning flight from Maui on the day of their birthday. Luckily, their birthday fell on a Sunday this year, so none of them had to miss any work because of the celebration. Because of the early arrival time of the Maui flight, they were able to begin the day by attending church together. Then she and Jack had spent the morning with Kimo, who insisted on fixing them an elaborate brunch.

At noon, the twins left for a busman's holiday, spending the afternoon at the Nani Mau Gardens just outside Hilo. Jack had a smaller cast now, reaching only from knee to toe, that made it easier for him to get around. They'd had a wonderful time, admiring all the beautiful plants and flowers. Even the brief shower that caught them outside at two o'clock couldn't dampen their pleasure in the day. They'd merely laughed, admired the rainbow it created, and continued their exploration of the gardens.

Now as she made the turn into their driveway, Ilima noticed the line of cars parked on the shoulder of the small road alongside their property. Surely Jack would notice too. She tried to think of an explanation she could offer, but her mind was blank.

She was still trying to think of something as she pulled slowly up the driveway, when Jack relieved her of the responsibility.

"The Tanakas must be having a party," he said. "Look at all the cars parked over by their place."

Ilima breathed a sigh of relief. The Tanaka family lived next door, just beyond the side street. It did indeed look as though they were entertaining a large group of friends. It was the perfect explanation for all the cars; she should have thought of it herself.

"Yeah, I noticed the cars."

Ilima was trying hard to act normal. But she was so excited about the surprise she had planned for Jack that it was hard to control her twitching mouth. Her lips wanted to spread into a grin, and she was sure Jack would know she was up to something.

But Jack didn't seem to notice anything unusual. In fact, he seemed a little excited himself. Probably looking forward to dinner with Kimo, Ilima decided.

She climbed out of the truck, stopping beside the passenger door to wait for Jack, who needed a little more time to manage the crutches.

Kimo must have been watching for them. As they started for the house, he opened the front door and waved.

"Hey, you two. Did you have fun?"

"It was great." Ilima could grin now without worrying about Jack's reaction. And she did. It was so good to see Kimo again, it would have been easy to laugh out loud, just for the sheer joy of it.

"Wait till you see the cakes I made."

"Cakes?" Ilima thought she'd heard wrong. Surely Kimo meant cake, singular. "You made just one for both of us, didn't you?"

"No."

Kimo was giving her his charming smile, showing his dimple, and she did love it. But surely two cakes were not necessary for the three of them and the handful of Jack's friends that she had invited.

"Everyone deserves their own personal birthday cake," Kimo declared. "I figure you two have had years of sharing a cake. It's about time you each had one of your own.''

He stepped aside, ushering them in the door before him.

It was almost laughable. Ilima wanted Jack to go in first, because of the people waiting to surprise him. Jack had picked this moment to be polite; he stayed back, wanting *her* to go in first. Because, of course, he knew her friends were waiting to surprise her.

Deciding they looked like a comedy act, Ilima finally stepped inside. She was glad to see Jack step in immediately behind her.

And then everything went crazy.

It sounded like a hundred voices yelling out, ''Surprise!'' People popped up from everywhere— the living room, kitchen, and hall, even their tiny office.

Ilima turned to see Jack's reaction, only to find him staring at her. Then they were surrounded by their friends, all laughing and talking at once. Not Jack's friends, Ilima finally realized. *Their* friends, both his and hers.

It took some time for things to settle down enough for Ilima and Jack to hear how the double party had come about. The noise level was high, and everyone was very proud of the way they'd pulled off the double surprise. The kitchen table was completely covered by the pot-luck offerings brought by the partygoers, with more spilling over onto the kitchen counters. A card table in the living room overflowed with brightly wrapped gifts.

And in a place of honor on the coffee table were two birthday cakes, one covered in chocolate frosting, one in butter cream. Kimo had decorated them as well, and not just with "Happy Birthday, Jack" and "Happy Birthday, Ilima." Jack's cake had a large bird of paradise drawn on the chocolate frosting. And on the white frosting for Ilima there was a yellow *'ilima* lei entwined with *maile*. The drawings were primitive but recognizable.

"My first time decorating a cake," Kimo told them. "What do you think?"

"Pretty good, man," Jack responded.

"They're beautiful." Ilima's voice was almost a whisper. She was so touched by the lovely cake, her eyes were damp with tears. Because Kimo had been right—the twins had always shared a birthday cake. This was the first time in her twenty-nine years that Ilima had had one all her own. "It's a wonderful present," she added.

"Hey, I got you a real present too," Kimo protested. "Here, let me get it."

He started toward the gift table, but was stopped by the objections of the guests.

"Eat first."

"Presents after eating."

"Birthday girl and boy first."

So Ilima and Jack were pushed toward the impromptu buffet table, paper plates thrust into their hands. Over their initial shock at having the double party, the twins got into the party spirit.

The food was excellent and abundant: platters and bowls of everything from noodles to sushi, fish cakes to teriyaki; sliced fruit sat next to fried chicken, boiled peanuts beside jiggling squares of colorful Jell-O. Soon everyone had a heaped plate, and competition was keen for chairs as well as for space on the living room floor.

The small house was completely filled. Ilima and Jack had pride of place on the living room sofa. Claiming the double party was his idea, so he deserved it, Kimo took up the third spot on the couch, right between the guests of honor. The other guests distributed themselves in the remaining chairs and all over the living room floor, spilling out into the hallway, even throwing open the front door and sitting out on the front stoop.

Conversation buzz filled the room to such an extent it drowned out the music Kimo had put on the stereo. But smiles and laughter indicated that everyone was having a good time. Kimo sat between his best friend and his best friend's sister, looking from one to the other. He felt like a spectator at a tennis match, but they were both so happy, he had to share in it. The double surprise party had worked better than his wildest dream.

Kimo moved his gaze to Ilima. She was talking to a girlfriend seated on the floor at her feet. Her mouth was parted in a smile, her eyes sparkling with happiness. He didn't hear what her friend said, but it caused Ilima to laugh. The musical sound insinuated its way through him, causing a ripple of pleasure that worked its way straight to his heart.

Kimo hadn't felt so happy in weeks, not since he'd returned to Maui after his short stay here. Nice as it was to be back in his own home, with his family, his heart had stayed behind in Puna with Ilima. He'd tried at first to deny it. But no matter what he was doing, a picture of Ilima—of her face, graced with a sad smile—kept intruding on his consciousness. He missed her intelligent conversation, her sensible approach to business. He missed her simple pleasure in his cooking, the way her eyes lit up when he surprised her with a special treat.

His eyes traveled around the room. For two people who claimed not to have many friends, they had packed the place.

Kimo shook his head. He'd contacted many of Jack's friends for Ilima. Jack had gotten in touch with a few of Ilima's friends who had then called others. Kimo had invited Mel Fernandez, who was there with his wife Denise and their newborn son. They were sitting near Jack, and he and Mel were discussing the accident and the arrests that had taken place.

"Hey, none of that now." Kimo tried a stern frown. "This is a party. You can't discuss that depressing business stuff."

With a grin Jack turned to his friend. "So what did you bring for Ilima? An engagement ring?"

Kimo realized that Jack was joking, but his famous poker face must have gone pale. Or something. Because Jack's grin widened until all his teeth showed, and he balanced his plate precariously on his good knee to hit Kimo on the back.

"You did! Congratulations, man."

"You'd better pipe down or you'll spoil the surprise," Denise told him. She sat on the floor beside her husband, their infant son between them in a carrier seat. She raised her eyebrows, a small movement of her eyes indicating Ilima sitting close by.

"Good point." Kimo was happy to get off this subject anyway. He was very nervous. Suppose Ilima didn't feel the same way he did?

Kimo glanced quickly over, noting that Ilima was speaking earnestly to her friend Sara from next door. He'd missed her so much these past few weeks, he'd hardly felt able to function. She, on the other hand, appeared to be continuing her life without any problems.

With his brooding inner thoughts taking him away from the festive party scene, Kimo went back to eating his dinner.

Beside him, Ilima turned from her friend Sara to find Kimo concentrating on his meal. She supposed someone as large as Kimo did need to keep up his energy. But she was disappointed. Maybe he hadn't missed her as much as she had missed him. She'd felt as though part of her life was missing after he left. Her life would never be the same. And he was eating.

"The food's great, isn't it?" Ilima said. "I can't thank you enough for going to all this trouble."

Kimo seemed to shake himself out of whatever thoughts had distracted him. "Ah, right. I wanted to do it."

His eyes met hers across their half-filled plates.

"For both of you."

Oh. Right. Ilima's heart fell. He'd done it for Jack. Of course. She picked up a cone sushi and took a bite.

Beside them, Jack started to say something, but stopped midword. He glanced back and forth between Kimo and Ilima. Both of them had set expressions. Both seemed to be giving a great deal of attention to their food. Jack set his plate down on the coffee table beside the cakes.

"Hey, I'm ready to open my presents. Is it time?"

Loud voices rose up around him, some yelling "yes," others saying they were still eating. Kimo finally stood, silencing everyone with a wave and a shout.

"Okay. How about if they start while you all finish eating. After all the gifts are open, we'll have cake."

This met with shouts of approval. He managed to organize enough hands to switch the gifts to the coffee table and the cakes to the card table. Then someone started Jack off by handing him a package.

The gifts were a pleasant combination of serious and fun. Jack got a bottle of liniment and some aspirin, but he also collected several nice T-shirts. And Kimo surprised him with a nice watch to replace the one that was broken in his accident.

Ilima's gifts tended to be on the serious side, but she did receive some sexy lingerie from two of her girlfriends, who told her that at her age, it was time for some serious man-hunting. The gift met with hoots of approval from the men present.

Finally, there was only one box left on the gift

table. It was on the small side, wrapped in silver foil and tied with a ribbon of iridescent blue.

Kimo rose to retrieve it, then handed it to Ilima with a serious expression. He had to force a smile. Darn, but he was nervous.

''This is for you, Ilima.''

The room had grown unnaturally quiet. The guests seemed to pick up on the tension sparking between Kimo and Ilima. After all the guessing and joking that went on during the previous openings, the sudden silence left her feeling as if she could hear the blood rushing through her veins. She took the small package with an unsteady hand. A jewelry box.

''What a pretty wrapping.''

Her voice was steadier than her hand, at least. She stared at the small box for so long someone shouted for her to open it. Others picked up the cry, and the party was back on track.

Ilima forced herself to slip off the ribbon. Then she turned the box over and pulled back the paper. She wasn't sure she wanted to open it. She wanted to continue to sit here and stare at the pretty bow and the silver foil and imagine what was inside.

As her fingers slid under the fold of the foil, her eyes rose to meet Kimo's. Back in his seat beside her, he was watching her with an intent gaze, but she couldn't tell what he was thinking.

Finally the paper fell away to reveal a gold box. It was obviously a jewelry box, but now Ilima was afraid she'd been dreaming her own impossible dreams. The box was too big for a ring. It was more of a size for a bracelet or earrings.

"You got X-ray eyes or something?" The shout came from one of Jack's friends at the back of the room, apparently impatient at her slow pace. "Open it already, so we can have cake."

Some of the women shushed him. "Let her take her time."

"Yeah, I'd savor every moment," added another female voice.

Ilima looked up, her eyes locking with her friend's. So she wasn't the only one thinking there might be a ring in the box. She glanced quickly around the room. All the women were watching with bright, eager eyes. The men, on the other hand, were beginning to turn hungry eyes on the cakes.

With the exception of Kimo and Jack. Kimo couldn't take his eyes off Ilima's face. His dark eyes were almost black with the emotion of the moment. But he couldn't bring himself to ask her to hurry.

And Jack . . . Ilima's twin brother watched with a hundred-megawatt smile on his face. Kimo had not confided in him, but he had a suspicion about that box. And he was delighted.

Ilima closed her eyes for one brief moment, then opened them and the box simultaneously.

At least it wasn't a bit of cotton inside, she thought. In the gold box was another velvet-covered jewelry box, which Ilima shook out into her hand.

"You got me some earrings."

She looked over at Kimo, her voice artificially bright. She didn't want to be disappointed, but it did look more like an earring box than a ring box. The ring boxes she'd seen were small and square, and usually made of black or white velvet. This box was smallish but rectangular, and emerald green. She had one very similar that held her good gold earrings—the ones Grandma had given her for her high school graduation. She ran her fingers lightly over the deep green velvet.

"Open it."

"Yeah, come on already. We're ready for cake."

A woman sitting next to the man who'd called out this last slapped him on the arm. "Let her alone."

Their friends took sides and hooted and called out, but Ilima and Kimo didn't hear a thing. Kimo was so serious, Ilima stopped with her fingers on the lid. Her eyes met his, and the smile left her face. His eyes showed little lines of strain, and his mouth was pulled so tight his dimple showed.

The room had turned silent again as the guests waited to see the last gift. Ilima heard a cardinal singing outside the window. The traffic noise was a dull throb that seemed to echo the sound of her blood rushing through her ears.

Finally she broke away from the intensity of Kimo's watchful gaze and opened the little velvet-covered box. It wasn't a pair of earrings. It wasn't a pin. It was a ring after all. A beautiful diamond, surrounded by red rubies.

Ilima stared at the ring in wonder. Her lips had parted, but no sound escaped her.

"I love you, Ilima." Kimo had slipped off the couch, and was down on one knee beside her. "Will you marry me?"

Ilima moved her eyes from the ring to Kimo. Tears were blurring her vision so that his face wavered in front of her. She threw her arms around his neck, the box still held in her hand, and breathed her reply somewhere in the vicinity of his left ear.

"Yes."

The shout that went up in the room around them must have scared the cardinal outside the window back to the farthest corner of the garden. Jack wrapped his arms around the both of them, and others were up and trying to add their congratulations.

"Wait!"

Kimo's shout managed to quiet them down some.

"I need to put my ring on her finger."

So the crowd around them retreated enough to allow Kimo the honor of placing the ring on Ilima's third finger. Hoots and catcalls demanded a celebratory kiss. Then they were swallowed up once again in the happy crowd. Hugs and kisses were exchanged. Champagne appeared for a special toast. Kimo had brought in a few bottles, then hidden them in the kitchen, telling Mel where to find them if needed. He'd tried to be optimistic. Happily, it had all worked out the way he'd planned.

Hours later, the party was over, the house covered with scattered cups and crumpled paper napkins that had to be disposed of before the ants found them. . . . But Jack pushed the happy couple out the door into the garden. They'd been surrounded by other people since their engagement, and he felt they deserved a few minutes alone.

Kimo led Ilima out toward the line of ti plants. As soon as they entered the shadows at the edge of the lawn, he pulled her into his arms for a kiss.

Ilima nestled against him. This felt so right. She

remembered the night two weeks ago when she'd snuggled into her afghan, imagining being held securely by Kimo, listening together to the rain on the roof. Now she'd have that chance.

Kimo ended the kiss and rested his cheek against Ilima's hair. He could smell the freshness of the rain and the richness of tropical flowers that lingered in her hair. And the feel of her lithe body against his brought out all the protectiveness he'd previously felt only with his young nieces and nephews.

Finally, he pulled back a little so that he could see her face. But his arms remained around her. He might never let her go.

"I thought about you all the time I was away."

"Oh, Kimo." Her sigh came from deep within. She was so happy here in his arms.

She brought her hand out and held it up before them, turning it slightly to catch the bit of light coming from the house. At the same moment, the moon moved out from behind a cloud, adding its silvery light to the sparkle in the ring. "It's such a beautiful ring."

"I thought of you the minute I saw it. It's like a bright flower, and I can't think of you without thinking of brightly colored flowers."

Ilima released her breath. "That's beautiful."

"I love you." Kimo's voice was soft. Gentle.

''I love you too.'' Ilima's voice was equally soft. Equally gentle.

''Can we still be friends?'' It was too dark to see his face, but Ilima could hear the smile in his voice.

''Of course. Husbands and wives should always be friends.'' She smiled as well.

Their voices mixed, high and low, as they both continued.

''Best friends.''